T
B[I]G
LIE

THE BIG LIE

A Shane Cleary Mystery

GABRIEL VALJAN

Contents

"The cruelest lies are often told in silence."

— Robert Louis Stevenson,
Virginibus Puerisque and Other Papers

"Knowing your own darkness is the best method for dealing with the darknesses of other people."

— Carl Jung,
Letter to Kendig B. Cully,
25 September 1931

Praise for The Big Lie

"Gabriel Valjan writes in a voice not heard since the golden days of the noir novel. His tough characters—good guys, bad guys, and confused folks just caught in the whirlwind—sparkle like the facets of a dark jewel, and his images linger in the mind after the book's long over."—SJ Rozan, bestselling author of *The Mayors of New York*

"If Raymond Chandler were alive today, this is the story he'd write: Great characters, a noir-ish plot that never flags, writing that sizzles, and a relevant tale of the ways in which justice is, sadly, not blind."—Mally Becker, Agatha-nominated author of *The Paris Mistress*

"Whip-smart, pacy, and full of curves. A worthy addition to the PI oeuvre."—Colin Campbell, acclaimed author of the Jim Grant thrillers

"When you begin a crime novel with PI Shane Cleary getting hired by a gangster to find a stolen pooch, a standard poodle named Boo, there are several ways you can go, and most of them are downhill. Fortunately, Gabriel Valjan is at the helm of *The Big Lie*, which guarantees it heads in the right direction. Up. The dialogue is snappy, the retorts witty, and along the way we meet a host of unforgettable characters—hey, it's Boston, what else would you expect?"—Charles Salzberg, award-winning and Shamus Award-nominated author of *Second Story Man, Canary in The Coal Mine,* and the Henry Swann series

Characters

- **Bonnie**: Shane's girlfriend and criminal defense attorney.
- **Delilah**: Shane's cat.
- **Tony Two-Times**: Bodyguard and associate of mafia don Mr. B.
- **Jim 'Jimmy' B**: South Boston gangster.
- **Delano 'Professor' Lindsey**: Shane's former teacher.
- **Israel 'Izzy' Duncan**: Bonnie's client.
- **Malcolm**: Dog groomer.
- **Brooklyn**: Street informant.
- **Seamus Costigan**: South Boston hoodlum.
- **Sean Costigan**: South Boston hoodlum.
- **Saul Fiedermann**: Jeweler in Shane's office building.
- **The Armstrongs**: Victims of jewelry theft, for which Israel Duncan stands accused.
- **John**: Shane's friend, and owner of a bar in Boston's Central Square.
- **Bill**: Friend of Shane, an Army veteran, and a Boston Police Department officer.
- **Noah**: Insurance fraud investigator.
- **Dot**: Dorothy at the Mercury Answering Service.
- **Tony Acosta**: A 'friend' of Bill's.
- **Butch**: Boston's Kenmore Square street musician.

Chapter One: Brother Rat

"A dog? You want me to find a dog?"

"That's right."

The head lifted, and eyes the color of Windex evaluated me. The slice of light from the streetlamp through the curtains behind him revealed a revolver on the armrest and a pair of pliers in one hand, which he squeezed to strengthen his grip. He used them to extract teeth from his victims. Whether he did it when they were alive or dead added to the legend and menace of Southie's most infamous son. Another man stood near him.

I'm told life serves you the same lesson over and over until you learn what you need to learn before the next thing comes along. I've also been told that karma never forgets an address. Jimmy was proof of both. He almost killed me but didn't. I should've killed him, but I couldn't because he was protected, and not by the mob. A stained badge shielded the man sitting in my chair, in my apartment in Union Park.

My landlady had called me at Bonnie's place. She told me I had visitors, and they wanted a word with me. She said Jimmy made a point of petting her two Corgis and offered her some advice. The thug recommended a brand of dog food, so her dogs wouldn't gain more weight. He emphasized canine physical fitness, which was pure Jimmy since he was a fitness nut.

Jimmy had muscles because, like most of the young lions in Southie, he lifted weights. He sported a veined neck, muscular arms, and a thick chest trapped inside a tight polo shirt. I knew if I couldn't take him, I was confident he'd feel me for days. We both weighed about 165 pounds, but I had a smidge more height than his five-eight. I had one more advantage over Jimmy: I

1

could stand my ground and take a hit. Jimmy, like most jockeys of the weight room, walked around with toothpicks for legs because he neglected to train them. His pant leg rode high enough for me to eyeball pasty shins, black socks, and sneakers. No ankle piece there.

I read the room as I came in. The situation would play out in one of two ways. One is someone pulled a trigger, and my last thought was either part of the hardwood floor or my brains were spaghetti against the wall and ceiling. The second option was I lived, forced to listen and learn how to avoid the same situation again. Like I said, a lesson in life and karma.

Jimmy murmured something to his bodyguard. It was low and slow, the kind of soft and secretive Irish whisper you'd expect in a bar's last hour. I assumed he'd told his man to wait outside because the guy moved past me. The door to my apartment opened and closed. I didn't see his face but caught a glimpse of the feet. Construction boots.

The pair of pliers indicated the chair near me. "Sit."

"I prefer to stand."

"Suit yourself."

I peeled my jacket off, so he'd know I was armed. His eyes admired the holster. I knew what he was going to say, so I said it before he did. "Same rig as Steve McQueen in *Bullitt*."

"Cross-draw don't seem bright or effective."

"Want to test me?"

His right hand pulsed with the pliers. A blued steel .357 slept on the left armrest of my favorite chair. His choice of firearm was an older model, not the kind Dirty Harry would carry, but it got the job done. Jimmy was right-handed, but that wasn't the point. His eyes flashed, as a way to taunt me, and then focused. "Nah, I don't feel lucky today, and all I want is for you to find my dog."

"On second thought," I said, "I think I'll take that seat."

"Excellent, we can have a civilized conversation then."

I get all kinds of crazy for clients because my retainer and daily rates are reasonable. Paranoid businessmen hire me because they suspect a partner or a favorite employee is a thief. Neurotic spouses hire me because they see a frequent flyer for a phone number on the bill from Ma Bell, or odd charges on their dearly beloved's statement from American Express. Bonnie told me family law was the worst, and I agreed, but it pays the bills.

I've listened to more sob stories and provided more free advice than Ann Landers. In short, I've handled embezzlement, fraud, infidelity, and, on occasion, missing persons, in addition to arson, murder, and narcotics. But this pitch to find a canine—a variation on a missing person or property—was new.

Jimmy, who didn't like to be called Jimmy, was an extortionist, a murderer, and South Boston's premier gangster, so it was hard for me to picture him heartsick over the absence of man's best friend.

He said, "Don't you have a cat?"

"Delilah."

"Delilah, that's right. You would be upset if she went missing, wouldn't you?" His hand waved, pliers and all. "There's a name...Delilah, as in Samson and Delilah. A female dog is called a bitch, but I never did learn what they called a female cat."

"A molly."

"You know, I've never cared for cats. Loyalty issues, moody and temperamental."

"Rather ironic coming from you. Cats are excellent judges of character."

"And what do you think your Delilah would say about me, if she could talk?"

"You wouldn't want to know. Can we wrap this up?"

Delilah, he didn't know, could talk. Sort of. She blinked once for Yes, twice for No, and meows were extra for emphasis. If she'd seen Jimmy now, she'd turn banshee and caterwaul profanities.

"You want me to find a dog?"

"A dog."

"Your dog?"

"My dog."

Jimmy had never been talky, or loud, but he commanded every room he was in with an unnerving silence. He neither drank nor smoked or used drugs. His mother was alive, and he looked after her like a doting son. His brother was successful on the other side of the tracks, in politics, and Jimmy went out of his way not to cast a shadow on *frater eius*.

"I'm aware that Shane Cleary doesn't need my money. I know he does all right as a landlord for his Greek friend, with steady income from tenants, and this PI thing is something he does for kicks, to try to make life interesting."

Those blue eyes sparkled in that truant light while he talked about me.

"Are you suggesting all that could vanish if I don't take the case?"

"Not at all," he said. "All I'm saying is I know things about you; things you might not know about yourself, things like personal history, and I don't mean your falling out with the Boston Police Department."

"Good to know, but I'm waiting for the other shoe to drop."

"You were too good for them, like you're too good to work for that dago in the North End."

"And there it is. I earn my money, and you know it, Jimmy."

"Yeah, you do. I had to say it before you tell me my money is no good."

"Money makes the world go round," I added.

"That's right. Money does, and it's all-American as apple pie."

"I know your story, and you say you know mine. What if I don't care what you know?"

"I do, and you will care about what I know. Speaking of I do, how come you haven't asked that lawyer broad you've been seeing to marry you?"

"She doesn't believe in marriage, and none of your business."

Jimmy was a career criminal and not someone I would associate with domesticity. Women close to him have disappeared, and yet there was little to nothing in his jacket for other misdeeds, thanks to his agent friend. Any priors going back to his teen years—like larceny, a spatter of robberies with a dash of assault and battery—was smoke on the water.

"Work this one case for me, Shane. It's all I ask. I'll pay you your rate and throw in the personal history as a bonus, if you'll find my dog."

"Personal history?"

"You haven't read or seen it. Trust me, this is something you don't know."

"You said it yourself. I don't need the money. As for your teaser about history …what if I don't care?"

He stared at me. He was Windex, and I was dirty glass.

"You will, I promise. That's your problem in life, Shane Cleary. You care, and this one time, Jimmy is gonna set you straight."

Jimmy was as volatile as a bucket of gasoline; he liked to test boundaries. All he needed was fumes and a lit match. Like the time someone called him Old Blue Eyes in one of the taverns on Broadway. The poor souse probably meant it as a compliment after one too many beers. Jimmy didn't see it that way. He especially hated Sinatra, the way he detested all Italians, so he stomped the guy's face in.

His eyes glanced down at the weapon under my arm. The holster was such that the gun pointed up at the armpit. His eyes met mine. "Did you know my old man lost an arm? Crushed between two rail cars. You would've liked him, Shane. He was a quiet, proud man, what we would call socially conscientious today. He'd clerk here and there at the Naval Yard, but he never worked a full-time job after he lost that arm."

"Tough break."

"Our fathers had something in common."

Being Irish was my first thought, but I waited for it through tight teeth. I wanted to punch him in the face for making any comparison between us. I thought I should've killed him when I had the chance. I wouldn't lose sleep over it, either.

"We're alike, you and I," he said.

"First the teaser and now, flattery. I'll bite. How do you figure we're similar?"

"We're both damaged. You came home from the war changed, like your old man."

I couldn't resist. "I went to Vietnam. What's your excuse?"

That made him smile and say, "Know how we're alike?"

"Don't know, Jimmy. Maybe some people would call us rats: me for my time with the BPD and you, well, you know."

His face didn't flinch or register emotion.

"We're alike because we both believe we're doing the right thing."

I waited for the rationalization, how what he was doing with the FBI helped South Boston, his people, the maligned Irish. Jimmy was a psychopath, and his line of thinking was a special aisle at Toys "R" Us.

"I'm doing my part to clear this town of those wop bastards. No different from you cleaning the stables at the Station House, like when you testified against that crooked cop."

"People within the department were crooked, Jimmy. He killed a black kid and staged the scene. There's a difference."

"'Potato, potahto, tomato, tomahto.' Say what you will. Call me an informant. A snitch. Call me a rodent with whiskers and sharp teeth, but go look in the mirror and tell me what you see, Brother Rat. Tell me how we're not alike."

"For starters, I was an only child. You weren't."

"You're right. My brother, the smart one, helped me as best he could, like that teacher, that professor helped you." He snapped his fingers. "What was his name?"

"Lindsey. Delano Lindsey."

"Did you know I taught myself the classics? I did it with a library card. See, we're both strong on initiative and self-education. You look to me like you're a man hot for Shakespeare. I bet you can quote something from the Bard. How 'bout it?"

"'The Prince of Darkness is a gentleman.' *Lear.*"

Jim wagged a finger. "That's good, but let's talk shop now."

"Talk about your dog?"

"No, personal history. Your old man went the way of Hemingway, didn't he?"

My blood rose. Several long seconds died between us, about the amount of time it took for one of Ray Guy's punts to land downfield.

"I'll let you in on something you didn't know about the day he did a Hemingway."

Through clenched teeth, I told him, "I know all I need to know about my father, thanks."

"Do you? 'To you, your father should be as a god.' *Midsummer Night's*

6

Dream."

Jimmy rose and took his jacket. He dropped the pliers into a pocket and hung the jacket over his left arm. He inserted the gun into his waistband behind him. I sat there numb, confused and intrigued. He said his man was outside, waiting in the car. Jimmy drove a black Mercury Grand Marquis.

He reached the door when, against my better judgment, I asked the question that betrayed my interest in the bait, his lure about personal history, "Where was the last place you saw the dog?"

"Roxbury. Dog groomer."

Jim rattled off the address while my mind tried to picture him dropping off his pet in the black section of town. I had to ask him. "This dog have a name?"

"Boo."

"As in *To Kill a Mockingbird.*"

"Righto."

"One last thing," I said. "Breed?"

"Poodle. Standard. Black. Studded collar. No tags."

Chapter Two: Tutor Wanted

Click. Click.

Out in the street, I heard the clicks of a cigarette lighter behind me. A profanity later, I see Tony Two-Times. He shook the lighter as if he thought a shift in the lighter fluid would help him scorch his lungs with the coffin nail.

"Problem, Tony?"

"This lighter is my problem, but it seems like the real problem just left your apartment."

"Thought you quit."

"Does it look like I quit?"

Jimmy was a gangster; Tony was a mafioso. Both men were killers, but, to Tony's credit, his victims were among his own, and seldom involved civilians. Jimmy killed on a whim. Tony did not. I walked towards him and the halo of smoke, once he torched his cig. I had to ask, "What brings you to my neighborhood?"

"More important question is, what brought that turd to your doorstep?"

I trod carefully. Tony expected an answer, but only his boss, Mr. B., and I knew the truth about Jimmy's protector. The old man knew better than to ice a federal agent because to do so would incur the unholy wrath of law enforcement and the federal government. Right or wrong, they'd bury him where he stood if he erased one of their own.

I offered Tony a half-truth. "He propositioned me."

Tony took a hit from the Marlboro Red. "Made you an offer, as in a job?"

"Yes."

"Considering it? You that hard up to take a gig from that piece of—"

"It's getting late, Tony. What can I do for you?"

"Answer my question first."

"Yes, he offered me a job, and no, I'm not hard-up. Satisfied?"

"Careful with the sarcasm. I like you."

"You're far from home, Tony. It's late, like I said, and I'm headed over to Bonnie's."

"I'll drive you."

"Here with something from your boss?"

He inhaled and exhaled smoke. "No, this one is from me."

"There's a first," I said and edited myself. "No sarcasm intended."

He smiled. "Get in the car. I'll drive and explain."

Mobsters drove either Lincoln Continentals or Cadillacs. The choice of car made me laugh. In Boston, the Italians disliked the Irish; the Jews disliked the Italians, yet both covered their furniture with plastic, and they decorated their homes in a color palette of baroque gold, rococo red, and earth tones. El Greco would have swooned. Blacks and Italians didn't get along either, and yet both groups favored the large cars, the fancy clothes, and the ostentatious jewelry.

The bolt popped, and I opened the door and climbed in. Unlike his brethren, Tony didn't trade in his wheels every year. Quite the contrary, this chariot was ancient, a 1975 Cadillac DeVille, its exterior Roxena Red with white stripe, with black Sierra Grain leather for interior.

Tony turned the key in the ignition. We sat there to let the car warm up. He asked after Delilah and Bonnie. I told him both were fine. Tony and Bonnie had hit it off. Which was unexpected and as odd a match as Felix Unger and Oscar Madison were for roommates. Tony was a criminal and Bonnie, a criminal defense lawyer. Crime was what they had in common, I told myself.

Tony pulled the gear out of park and angled the nose of his tank for Tremont Street. There was no radio on, no nothing, except the sound of the engine and the smoke from his cigarette. My finger found the button, and I cracked the window for fresh air and oxygen.

Tony's hand, on his side of the car, used the master control and closed the window on me. I looked at him, and he told me, "I don't want to catch a cold."

"Second-hand smoke is as dangerous as smoking itself."

"Then don't inhale."

"What's this about Tony?"

"What did that nutcase want?"

"He wants me to find a dog."

The end of his cigarette reddened and relaxed into a soft hue of orange. "A dog?"

"Poodle."

"A poodle?"

"May I open the window, Tony, because I think there's an echo in here."

"I always figured him for a Rottweiler, but a poodle?"

"If it is any consolation, it's a standard poodle, and not one of those small floor mops."

"Hate those things, and Chihuahuas, too. Ankle-biters and neurotic."

Chihuahuas were a favorite with the Spanish, but Tony didn't use the words Hispanic or Latino when he talked about them. He was an equal opportunity offender when he talked about Chinese and Jewish people as well. While we waited at a red light, I inquired again as to why he had graced me with his presence. Bonnie lived a short distance from where we idled in nonexistent traffic. I could've walked it, but it would've been unhealthy to say no to Tony Two-Times.

He could've run the light, and nobody would've known. Laws of traffic, he obeys, while others of God and Man he broke.

"I need you to come up to the Lake. I need your help with something personal."

By 'the Lake,' he meant where he lived, Newton, more specifically Nonantum, one of the thirteen villages of what Bostonians lumped together and labeled Newton. Some referred to Nonantum as Silver Lake, but the loyal and fierce natives called it 'The Lake.' You could hear the capital letters. Of course, the first thing I pictured in my head with the word 'lake' was Fredo inside a small boat in the second *Godfather*. 'Personal' rang like tinnitus.

"Can you be specific by what you mean when you say 'help' and 'personal'?"

"Help as in Latin. You know Latin?"

"I'm rusty. Why?"

"Professor friend of yours, he knows Latin, right?"

"He taught it for years before the incident."

We both understood the euphemism. Delano Lindsey had lost his job after he was accused of an inappropriate relationship with a student. It was a bum rap with no merit, but it was one of those baseless accusations that did more damage without proof. The alleged student wasn't a student, and either way, Delano received the academic wingtip.

Tony tapped some ashes into the ashtray. "What about Bonnie?"

"What about Bonnie?"

"She knows Latin, right? She's a lawyer. Lawyers know Latin."

"She knows enough for the law. What's this about Tony?"

"My niece. She is struggling with Latin, and my mother asked me to find the kid help."

"Niece explains why it's 'personal' to you. Why don't you talk to Bonnie?"

"Because I'm talking to you."

"You get on well with Bonnie. You can ask her yourself."

Tony exhaled smoke. "That's not how things are done. I'm talking to you because I need to know it's okay with you before I make this request."

I imitated the priest and blessed him. "*Pax vobiscum. Ite in pace.* Happy now? That was Latin for 'Peace be with you. Go in peace.' Go ask her yourself, my son."

"You're a regular comedian, Cleary."

"If asking a woman dents your machismo, I could tutor the kid. I know Latin better than Bonnie does."

"You can't. This is an Italian thing."

Tony had said it cold, hard, and with a tone that was definitive.

I digested the rejection. "Oh, I get it."

"No, you don't, Cleary."

"We've resorted to last names now. Is that an Italian thing, too?"

I waited for a reaction and nothing until, "Is what Italian?"

"You ask me, and then I ask Bonnie."

"Yes and no."

We moved through the night while I processed his response. When I dealt with Mr. B, everything was discussed in code, a second language, because the man was paranoid about surveillance, about bugs planted in his home, at his social club, and in public places. Here, I was in Tony's car, and I was happy some things didn't change and happier the car hadn't gone up in an explosion when he turned the engine over.

I pushed the issue. "It's one or the other, yes or no, Tony."

"You're not creative, are you? I mean, you can't entertain two conflicting thoughts at once. You know, the most dangerous individual is the person who views the world as either black or white. That's why I like animals, they see the world, in shades of gray."

"An insult and philosophy," I said. "Want me or Bonnie to tutor this kid, or what?"

"I prefer Bonnie. I know rejection is hard, but you'll recover."

"So much for equality between the sexes. You want her, but you won't ask her?"

"Yes, and I'll pay you."

I stared through the glass in front of me, took in the play of streetlights and glare.

"I think you need to rethink economics, Tony. You pay the person who does the job."

He looked at me as if I had insulted him. "What's wrong with you?"

"What do you mean what's wrong with me? If Bonnie does the job, you pay her."

Nobody was on the street, but Tony jerked the car to the curb. I had said something wrong, and he'd turned serious. He jammed on the brakes, slammed the car into park, and shifted in his seat to face me.

"Think it through, Cleary. She's a lawyer, and I'm not one of her clients. If I pay her, the Massachusetts Bar Association wouldn't look so kindly on that relationship."

"Makes sense," I said. "I'm impressed. If you want to circumvent the problem altogether, why not have your sister or your brother pay her?"

"Don't bring my sister into this. I've got enough agita in my life."

"Okay, we've established your sister is the girl's mother. What about her father?"

"Sister is divorced, and he's MIA. There isn't enough Alka-Seltzer for me to explain the family dynamic, and no cracks, please, on family and him missing. The bit that's Italian is simple. My mother and my sister are against a man teaching her. It's complicated."

The concern here was propriety. The Italian family wanted a woman for a female student because a strange man coming to the house invited speculation, and innuendo would damage the young lady's reputation. I wanted to offer a solution, but I had to confirm a detail first.

"This niece of yours, she goes to a Catholic school?"

"Yeah, how did you know?"

"You're kidding, right? The number of vowels in your last name tipped me off."

"Yeah, she does. Andrea attends Sacred Heart. Why?"

"Go to the local convent and find yourself a nun who knows Latin. Problem solved."

"Are you nuts? Penguins are the worst. Those broads are nuts."

"You're something, Tony, you know that? I'll see what I can do. I'll talk to Bonnie."

"Thank you." He pulled the car out of park, into the sparse traffic, and drove the few blocks to Bonnie's apartment. Instinct told me there was more to come from my chauffeur, but I hit him with another question. "Why don't you bring Bonnie to the Lake?"

"I need to bring you to the Lake first."

"Let me see if I've got this right. You want me to ask Bonnie because you won't?"

"Yes."

"I get why you want to pay me instead of her, but you can't bring her to the Lake?"

"Correct. I need to talk to my mother first. My niece and sister live with my mother."

"And you want me to go with you to the Lake?"

"Correct again."

I'd forgotten Tony enacted a monthly penance with his mother for moving out of her home. The woman perceived it as a betrayal. It didn't matter that he lived a few blocks away from her. His acts of contrition included pastries from Antoine's Bakery. He also atoned for another offense against *materfamilias* because he had married a girl from Naples and not Sicily. Ma equated his matrimonial decision, his choice of lifelong mate, with an interracial marriage.

He eased the car in front of the house. My fingers on the door handle, I said to Tony, "You need your mother's approval. Will that be all this evening?"

"What nationality is Bonnie?"

"What?" The question startled me.

"Her nationality? What is she?"

This was so Bostonian, so typical of the East Coast, it never occurred to me that it was offensive to ask someone what they were or what they did for a living until I stepped away from the Commonwealth of Massachusetts. Stranger to me was when I encountered guys in the army who'd never seen a black person until Basic Training.

"She's a mutt like most Americans, Tony. You know her last name."

"Loring, so what? It doesn't tell me where her people are from."

"Does it matter?"

"It matters to my mother."

"You're serious."

"I don't joke about my mother."

"Is it because it's her house, or is it because you're afraid of her?"

"Both. How do you think I got this way? Trust me, you'd rather deal with me than her."

"She's that tough, huh?"

"You've heard of Machiavelli, right?"

"Don't tell me he's required reading in your profession."

"I've got this theory that Machiavelli was a broad, like how some people think Shakespeare was a woman. Think about it, Niccolò could easily have been Nicole or Nicoletta. Only an Italian woman could've written *The Prince.*"

I shook my head and asked if we were done. When Tony didn't say anything, I stepped out and closed the door. I couldn't resist the temptation and tapped the window and waited for him to lower it.

"What is it?"

"When and where do we meet once ma grants a visitor's pass?"

Tony answered, "Where is easy enough. Caffé Vittoria. You know it?"

"On Hanover Street. When?"

"I'll call your answering service when I know and talk to what's her name."

"Dot."

"That's what I said."

"You have Dot's number?"

"I just said I did if I plan to call her and don't forget to discuss the thing with her."

"You mean Bonnie?"

"Who else?"

"Right," I said. "I'll talk to Bonnie, and I'll visit the land of mortgages and Mercedes with you. And one more thing, Tony."

"What?"

"Roll up the window. I wouldn't want you to catch a cold."

"One last question for you," he said. I waited for it. "What's with keeping the old apartment when you live here with Bonnie? You allergic to commitment or something?"

"Go home, Tony. My cup runneth over."

I walked away, perturbed and disturbed that twice in one night, I was reminded of my marital status, that I was both juvenile and afraid of responsibility. It made me feel stupid as a Muppet.

Chapter Three: Pro Bono

Next morning, I woke up to the aroma of coffee, the sputters and crackles of eggs and bacon in the skillet, and the loud ping of the toaster downstairs. Half awake, my brain tried to think as Bonnie walked into the room in a tailored blue suit and white blouse, a breakfast tray in front of her. I pulled myself up into a sitting position along with the bed sheet.

"Hope you don't mind. I brought up a package for you," she said.

A manila envelope landed inside the small valley formed between my legs. No metered or cancelled stamps in one corner or return address in the other, but one of my business cards had been taped center stage to save someone the time from having to write my name and details. I undid the metal pincers to open it.

I pulled out the contents. Hundred-dollar bills. Fifty of them. A small picture had fallen out with them. I examined the cardboard stock, a Kodak moment of Boo. *Canis lupus familiaris.* Jimmy had neglected to mention the red collar and metal studs. Boo had angled his or her head for the camera. The eyes were expressive, intelligent, with a hint of mischief in them.

I fanned the money. Five grand was some serious green for me as dogcatcher.

Bonnie returned with a side of buttered toast to accompany the eggs and bacon.

She worked at a prestigious law firm, and prestige allowed her some indulgences, like the Jamaica Blue Mountain coffee from Cardullo's in Harvard Square. Not all was Mike and Carol Brady between us. She once underwent physical therapy after a beating meant as a message to me. Another time, she was upset that I wasn't forthcoming about my time in the army. We patched the potential hole in our relationship and promised to be honest with each other. I helped her with her cases when she asked, and I let her know as much as she needed to know about my cases since she was a lawyer and wanted to keep her law degree safe and sound inside its frame.

She'd seen the money. "Generous client."

I opened up the napkin for my lap and picked up the fork. I thanked her for breakfast. I gave her a fast flash of teeth for a smile and avoided eye contact.

"Hefty retainer says desperate client. Sounds like a big case. Care to share?"

"It's too early for the cross-examination, Counselor."

"Remember," she said. "Honesty is more than a song from Billy Joel."

I prevented egg white from falling with my left hand.

Bonnie stood out tall and blonde in the crowd of dour and sour Bostonians. Once upon a time, her Scandinavian ancestors roamed and raided up and down the coast of England. Long before Henry VIII, they had plundered the abbeys for the gold and precious jewels used to decorate books in the scriptorium. A thousand years later, her livelihood depended on volumes few people understood or read. Bonnie was fierce and tenacious, in and out of the bedroom.

"What's the case?" she asked.

"Thought your kind believed in client confidentiality?"

"My kind? Don't be an ass and talk like Don Rickles."

"Don Rickles?"

"Don't insult me when you can love me."

She crawled across the sheets, a smile on her face. One hand reached, nails done in pink and French manicured, her lips landed first on my neck and then moved to my ear. I didn't look, but I felt her warm breath and then the slightest pinch as she bit my earlobe. I shivered. When she pulled back, she said the most dangerous words, "I need a favor."

My head turned, and her lips touched mine without disturbing her lipstick. I would've turned on a hip, but I remembered the breakfast tray and set it to the side. I moved in for a more committed kiss, but her hand pushed me

17

back against the pillow. "Don't get ahead of yourself, Marlowe. Hear me out first," she said.

I rested against the pillows. Delilah, near my feet, yawned with a loud display of incisors.

"Lay it on me."

"I was wondering whether you'd do a little investigating for me."

She settled into a half-moon next to me. I saw some leg. When she wore a dress, Bonnie didn't believe in modern hosiery. No L'eggs pantyhose for her. She was old school, all about the silk, including the lace garter belt.

"What did you have in mind?"

"The firm is doing some pro bono work."

"Lawyers with humanity and a conscience. There's a concept."

"Aren't you the cynic?" Her fingers visited my chest.

"You've been assigned a pro bono case. Tell me more."

"Disadvantaged kid from a rough neighborhood. A terrible lapse in judgment early on."

I asked her, "How early on?"

"Before he was twelve. Why? Everyone deserves a second chance."

"Okay, you sold thirty seconds of ad space. Give me the remaining thirty seconds. Middle-aged men have lapses in judgment, and often with a dish half their age. Disadvantaged kids commit crimes, and if they're black or Latino, the book is thrown at them, hard, and time inside the system makes them worse criminals. What did he do?"

"Arrested for stealing."

"Is that past or present, or both?

"Both," she said. "I should have waited for a better time to talk to you about this."

"Now is as good a time as any. What did he steal?"

"Jewelry, both times. Why?"

"It establishes a pattern. The rest, please."

I drank a small sip of the Jamaican coffee. Her eyes were on me. She had crossed her arms in front of her. I'm closed off and in control here, her body said as our eyes met. Lawyers like to think of themselves as surgeons of

18

logic, but they've never experienced the box on the receiving end of a police interrogation. Cops, active or retired, see facts differently, through a certain filter, the way a photographer sees light and shadow.

I said, "Let's restart this conversation. What did he steal?"

"Jewelry," she said. "Your read of the situation, Mr. Cleary?"

"First time he stole jewelry, it had to be something cheap. Am I right or wrong?"

"Pair of earrings, and you're right. Woolworths on Washington Street. Why?"

"Because the ante starts at grand theft, for his case to have landed at your firm. His five-finger discount was worth over a thousand bucks, true or false?"

"True, and way over a thousand."

"Felony theft it is," I said. "Let's discuss mitigating circumstances."

"What mitigating circumstances?"

"There's an angle here somewhere; firms don't take on cases they don't think they can't win. Witnesses?"

"Sort of."

"Priors?"

"Told you earlier. Juvenile record."

"Right," I said and put my hand to my head imitating the bumbling Columbo, who wanted his suspects to think he was inept and an idiot. "I forgot about that 'lapse of judgment.'"

"Why are you being such an ass?"

"Because when a frat rat or some wealthy legacy student rapes a girl, opposing counsel suggests the amount she drank was a 'lapse of judgment.' He boosted earrings from a store, and that's shoplifting, but felony theft suggests a move from the minor to the major leagues, pun intended. Felony theft suggests to me a B&E with premeditation." I repeated Columbo's hand-in-the-air gesture. "Answer this: Is he black or Hispanic?"

"What's race got to do with it, Shane?"

"Everything. You said 'disadvantaged kid.' Breaking and Entering, or not?"

"Yes, a B&E."

"Black or Latino?"

"Black." Her hands dropped into her lap. I reached for them. I squeezed them. I wanted to see her eyes. She wouldn't look up.

"Now, here's the most important question, Bonnie." I waited until her eyes met mine. For a second, they did. "You've been working contracts these last few months, and now you've been assigned a criminal case, pro bono." My hand pulled her chin up. "What does that tell you?"

Bonnie was intelligent, smarter than I was every day of the week, including Sunday, but that didn't mean she was confident every month of the year. As a lawyer, she could outwit half the associates with their fancy briefcases from Helen's Leather Shop on Charles Street and a few of the partners with diplomas from Harvard Law and the London School of Economics, but she was inexperienced with office politics.

She was learning realities and appearances. Pro bono was public relations, politics, and a byline in the professional journal or the newspaper, and worth about as much as a drink at the neighborhood bar, so long as the watering hole was on Beacon Hill.

Her eyes, a different shade of blue from Jimmy's, stared into me.

"Here's how I see it. They came to you with this case. Slam dunk, they might've said. Take a break from contracts, they said. Get back to criminal law, which you love, they told you. They say it's pro bono, do it and it'll put you in good with the partners. You could protest and say you're rusty on criminal law because you're the contracts gal now. They increase the charm and pour you a glass of Chardonnay and remind you it's all procedural, open and shut. How am I doing?"

"Martini," she said softly. "They gave me a martini."

Her blank expression tightened.

"Open and shut means plead the kid out and be done with it, and call it justice."

Bonnie rose and took the breakfast tray. Another reason I could never be a lawyer. A win shouldn't make a person feel like crap. Bonnie may have had an ulterior motive for serving me breakfast in bed, but I was sending her into the day defeated and downbeat. I called out to her. She turned.

"They don't have their own investigators?"

"They do, but they said there was little to no budget for this case."

"Which means I'm working this case pro bono, too. I have a request." She stood there and glared at me as if I had tracked mud throughout the house. "I have a favor of my own."

Delilah's head lifted. She did this when she suspected humans couldn't hear or smell like her, and according to her, I was guilty of something foul to both senses. Her ears twitched, and she settled into a question mark of tail wrapped around her legs. Her eyes considered us, and she blinked.

"You have a favor?" she asked.

"I do. You could call it quid pro quo."

"Quid pro quo? If this is about sex, you really know how to make a girl feel like a—"

"No sex," I said.

I had offended her. "Let me guess. Someone is cooking dinner all week?"

"God, no, not cooking."

"Shane Cleary, you're through the ice, and I'm about to watch you drown or freeze to death, whichever happens first. You started the negotiation process, so put something on the table."

"I will," I said and leaned back into the pillow behind me. "How's your Latin?"

"Enough to know that quid pro quo means this for that."

"But not enough to know the phrase doesn't exist in the entire canon of classical literature."

"What do you mean?" she asked, still holding the tray. "It's Latin."

"No, it isn't. Quid pro quo is an invention."

"'An invention?'" She had cocked her head like Delilah would when she heard something at the subsonic level, but I didn't want to overstate the point. Bonnie may be the spread to my bread, but play this wrong, and she'd stab me with the butter knife. I'd make the explanation short and to the dull point.

"Quid pro quo is made-up Latin. The original phrase is *Qui pro quo*, and that means 'misunderstanding,' while the actual Latin phrase for 'this for that' is *Do ut des*, which is ironic, don't you think?"

She placed the tray down on the edge of the bed. "I'll play along since I need your help. How is it ironic?"

"Translate *Do ut des*."

She understood that I was testing her Latin, for reasons unknown.

"The phrase comes from Roman contract law."

"Translation, please, Counselor."

Her lips twisted. I amused her. She delayed her response for effect, but I wouldn't repeat my question. She'd make me work for it. I'll admit that it was not unlike foreplay before the riot of sex. I caved and asked, "What does the phrase mean in English?"

"I give so that you may give. Now tell me what this is all about."

"Tony's niece is having trouble with Latin. She needs a tutor."

"And Tony approached you?" She looked perplexed. Her forehead creased. "We both know Delano is the better choice. Oh, wait, his past, with that student."

"That did come up," I said.

"My Latin is limited to case law."

"I said the same thing."

"Wait, you know Latin better than I do. Why don't you tutor her?"

"Same reason Delano can't."

"You're guilty of rug burns because you rode some girl on the carpet behind the desk?"

"An image of Delano I didn't need inside my head, but the answer is no. The reason why is that Delano and I are the wrong gender. It seems, for reasons too complicated to discuss now, Tony's mother thinks a male tutor is inappropriate."

"His mother?"

"You forget this is Tony we're talking about. Let me save you some time. Tony and I agreed there can't be any connection between you and him, which is why his mother is paying me for your services. Wait." I held up a hand. "There's more. I'm to meet his mother."

"You get paid, but I tutor the kid?"

It was my turn to fold my arms in front of my chest. "Yes, I'm the bag man."

"In what universe does any of this make sense?"

"In Tony's world, called the Lake. Do we have a deal?"

Chapter Four: Dots

A ferocious German shepherd, a snapping Doberman, and a snarling pit bull were what I paired with Jimmy. Steinbeck, the novelist, traveled the country in a camper with his standard poodle, Charlie. Same dog, except Jimmy drove a black Mercury Grand Marquis.

My quest for the address on the piece of paper in my hand began on the Washington Street Elevated into Dudley Square. Roxbury, like most of Boston, had a storied past. William Dawes, the other half of Paul Revere's famous midnight ride, started his horse trot here. Rocksberry became Roxbury, and finally, The Berry, to the natives. White flight would bequeath the neighborhood to black folks for most of the twentieth century. A transplant from Omaha, Nebraska named Malcolm X would live on Dale Street with his half-sister. My destination was a side street off Dudley Street.

No matter how I dressed, I stank of white to the locals. Eyes were on me. Two teenagers, not Boy Scouts, warmed their hands over a campfire of flames inside an oil drum. I passed long-vacant lots filled with broken glass, scrap metal, and other debris. Weeds and trash everywhere, and silence, too. I turned down the street to find my number.

There was a porch, one side sunken where the termites had laid siege. Dogs yelped, so I knew this was the right place. It got quiet when I approached the door. The dogs had sensed me, gotten a whiff of my scent. I could cup my hands and peer in the window, but I knew better. A white man on the stoop was enough to warrant a violent response in this neighborhood. I rapped the door twice. Everyone behind a curtain on this block heard that knock before my knuckles touched wood.

All the television shows get it wrong. The car or foot chase isn't dangerous; it's the simple act of walking up to a door. Entering a house is a different matter because you don't know what awaits you on the other side of the wood. Home is a sacred space to most Americans. The Second Amendment's right to defend oneself is as ingrained and primitive as the pioneers' divine right to kill every Indian they met.

The door opened into a room with several high tables. I took slow and decisive steps. Different breeds of dog stared at me, wide and wet-eyed, curious and afraid. Small leashes tethered them to small stations. I spotted clippers for fur, clippers for nails, but no sign of humans. Not one dog made a sound.

I announced my name. I said I wasn't a cop and was there to talk. I said I had a simple question about the whereabouts of a poodle named Boo. The query provoked something. A figure shot out from a back room for the rear door. Once flung open, light flooded the room, and the dogs became agitated. They barked, whimpered, and circled inside their cages as if someone had come for them to do the canine version of the long and final walk to the death chamber.

I thought I had him, but he decided he'd do sprints and hurdles over trash barrels like Jesse Owens. I followed him, up and over one fence, down another alley, up a small hill, through clothes on the line in another backyard, and across a driveway where a driver jammed on the brakes like Fred Flintstone. I skittered across the hood of the car, only to catch a wet bag of trash in the chest. I ducked when a metal lid was thrown at my head. He kept going. I kept chasing. We ran down a valley of a street before it turned into a steep hill. I could hear him panting, and I knew he could hear me behind him. He tripped over something, thank God, and tried to crawl. I fell to my knees and made a feeble attempt at tackling him. I grabbed some of his wet shirt and took him down to the ground. We both hungered for air, as if we shared one lung.

"Stop," I gasped. "For the love of God, stop."

He rolled over onto his back. I did the same. We were equal under the sun.

"What do you want, man?"

"The...the dog. I want...to know about the poodle. Boo."

"What's to know," he said through his own wheezing. "Two scary dudes picked him up."

"What two dudes?"

"How the hell do I know," he said. "Think I asked to see ID? I assumed the boss man couldn't pick Boo up, and they were his boys."

I felt as if I could breathe through my eyes. My brain tried to think while my lungs burned. "Has someone in his crew picked up Boo before?"

"Yeah," he said. He righted into sitting. He was the hare, and I was the tortoise trying to find my shell. He reached over and gave me a hand to help me up.

"Thanks. Name is Shane."

"Malcolm."

"Tell me, Malcolm, these guys weren't regulars, were they?"

"Nah, man. Not regulars. First time I'd ever seen 'em."

"Then why did you give them the dog?"

I used a hanky from a back pocket to wipe the sweat from my forehead and my neck.

"If you know the dude who owns the dog, then you know he's one scary mother...point is, when these guys showed up, I didn't ask questions. Dig?"

"I do, but why did you run?"

"Figured you worked for the man."

"I do."

"Shit, I shoulda kept running."

"It's not what you think."

"Let me ask you something, man."

"Go ahead." I tucked away my handkerchief and waited for the question.

"I handed off the dog to the wrong guys, didn't I?"

"Yep."

"Fuck me."

Malcolm dusted himself off. I had another question. "These guys—other than being big and scary—anything you can tell me about them? See their car?"

26

"I didn't see no car, but yeah, big and scary about covers it, and they were as Irish as the leprechaun on a box of Lucky Charms cereal." Malcolm used hands to signify height and weight. "One more thing I noticed about them. Both of them had dots."

"Dots?"

He turned his hand over and bared the soft side of his wrist.

"Each of 'em had a dot there. Does that mean something among you white folks?"

"Yeah, let's walk together."

We did. I wanted to laugh, but it came out somewhat strangled.

I told him the truth. "It's called the Southie dot."

"Special kind of crazy Irish, huh?"

I proved to myself that I'd been hanging around Tony too much because I said, "Yes and no."

Chapter Five: Irish Squeeze

The T beneath the Boston Common was never pleasant. Poorly lit and ventilated, Beantown's subway, first in the nation, had crowds on the platform and rats on the rails. Every day except for the odd schedule on Sundays, humans and rodents scurried to their destinations.

I got off the MTA at Central Square and crossed Mass Ave to John's Place. A bus gasped and wheezed to a complete stop. People exited, and the bus belched a black cloud. Mass Ave was alive with record stores, thrift stores, used bookstores, an occasional eatery, and bars.

Like his jazz, John was always the experimentalist in business. In the winter, the interior of his establishment was brighter than the sun in July, and in the summer, dark as a December day. He had this theory. John always had one. Some article in *Psychology Today* discussed sunlight and hormones, which John said the shrinks correlated to eat and drink and changes in moods. I don't know. I thought people drank because they enjoyed the brotherhood of the grape. I stepped into John's Place for the sounds of Brubeck and Coltrane. I came today for any worthwhile word on the street. Other than a priest, a barkeep was the next best thing, without the vows getting in the way.

Two men were sitting at the far end, beers in one hand and their other mitt in a bowl of nuts. I could hear them slur their way through the hills of nostalgia. Past was past, and then John stood in front of me. Massive chest and enormous arms, John stretched out the Hanes white t-shirt like a black Mr. Clean. He worked the counter space with a dishcloth. He polished the wood until the squeaks stopped.

John and I enjoyed this game we called Reversal. I'd act the part of the weary traveler desperate for a drink, and he'd play the racist who didn't like my kind in his bar. It wasn't far from reality since I was often the only white person in his place.

"Guinness, please," I said and parked myself on a stool.

John didn't say a word. His features were fixed in a hard mask, and his eyes shone hostile. He'd pass for the actor John Amos, the father on the TV show *Good Times*. He picked a glass and started pulling a pint. He did it the way any self-respecting barman would in Dublin. The stout beer darkened the glass. Eyes watched us from all the corners of the room. I decided to kick it off by violating the universal law around drinking Guinness. I touched the pint before he handed it to me.

"What are you doing?" he asked.

My hand covered his, like ivory over ebony or paper beats rock.

"I'm thirsty," I said.

"The foam has to be right. Sure you're Irish and not the milkman's kid?"

I spruced my response and made it sound as if I were offended and said something about maternity, paternity, and plantations. Behind us, a game of pool halted. When I came in, balls were clattering and smacking around the felt. Men were calling shots, collecting their bets, and chalking their sticks.

In a voice loud enough to worry mice, John said, "You some kind of redneck Irish?"

"No less than one generation away from sharecropper, and you're uppity. All because you own this hole in a wall."

"Did you call me uppity?"

"I stand corrected," I said and slapped the counter. "You're one of them cosmopolitan coloreds."

"What's a woman's magazine got to do with anything, you mick son of a bitch?"

John had planted both fists on the counter. Whether it was the Coltrane song or Cornell Woolrich story, "Night Has a Thousand Eyes" played overhead as the perfect companion piece to our little performance. John clenched his jaw. He flexed his chest. Everyone in the place behind me, including the two drunks at the other end, held their breath. I tried to keep a straight face until John made one pectoral jump and then the other. Then we busted out laughing.

Someone cursed. Someone else called for a fresh rack and a game of rotation pool.

"What brings you around, man?" John asked.

"How's Silvia?"

"Wife is good. Business is good. Sil is cooking up a storm these days, and she's got Lindsey and me fed and fattened up like hogs. You ought to stop by sometime."

We talked, and I noticed John worked the same section of counter again and again with his cloth. "What's bothering you, John?"

"Nothing. I said everything was good. Why?"

"You've polished the same spot of wood four times."

"Yeah, I forgot you notice everything, except what's important."

"What did I miss?" I asked.

"Bonnie, for one thing. Oughta put a ring on that girl before she loses patience with you."

"Not you, too."

"Huh?"

"Never mind," I said and tapped the wood. "What is it?"

"Nothing I want to bother you with." I reached over and put my hand on top of his. The whites of his eyes glistened, and he leaned forward for a close conversation. He relented and explained what ailed him. "You recall how a certain Mediterranean gentleman had convinced certain people not to bother me anymore?"

I moved my hand. "You can say Irish scum, John. I won't take offense."

I could count the blood vessels in his eyes. "The Irish scum are back. I didn't want to bring it up because I know the man has had his own set of problems."

In the not-so-recent past, Mr. B survived a coup fomented and fermented by a coalition of Canadian mafia, Jimmy's Winter Hill Gang, and a cadre of Puerto Ricans looking to make a profit from cocaine and use a part of the proceeds to fund a radical political group on the island. I'd warned Mr. B that the Feds were not far beyond, and he should retire while there was air in his lungs. He didn't, and he wouldn't. I survived the confrontation with Jimmy's protector, and my friend Hunter helped put people in the graveyard.

A whistle summoned John for a refill. John excused himself and rode his white cloth down the grain of wood until it stopped in front of his customer. He filled the order, returned, and continued the conversation.

"Believe me when I tell you, I'm not asking you to solve this problem or stick your head where it don't belong. I'm grateful, more than grateful, but if this nonsense persists, then there'll be trouble. I ain't got no problem introducing those boys to John Brown, but what I worry about most is harassment from the po-lice."

When John said John Brown, he didn't mean the abolitionist at Harper's Ferry. When we first met, John acquainted me with the business end of a Browning shotgun. I'd been the faster draw, but we resolved our misunderstanding and were friends ever since. Back then, he had mistaken me for another Irish thug doing morning collections. John was a businessman, a black businessman, and an honest one who didn't tolerate drugs or pimps on his property, which didn't stop the Irish, the Italians, and crooked cops from preying on him. The Italians controlled the liquor shipments and took a percentage. The Irish wanted to control the vending machines. The cops wanted to skim whatever cream was left over and call it protection.

John described his visitors to me. The two goons matched the descriptions Malcolm gave me, down to the dots on their wrists. Problem was every Southie delinquent wore that mark of Cain. It was either the dot on the inner wrist or a pinpricked Shamrock. Hardly original, hardly distinctive in an Irish neighborhood, and Malcolm mentioned their hairstyle, which was hair parted down the middle and winged back on the sides. Another Southie trademark.

"Catch the name for these two?"

"Costigan," John said. "Sean and Seamus."

"Pay them?"

"Hell no, but something tells me they'll be back, and the conversation will get ugly. For now, it's all talk, the usual jive threats, like my shipments might get lost, might fall off of a truck, a window might get broken, and a fire might happen. It's a familiar song to black folks, and the tune goes, might rhyme with white."

"I'll talk to our mutual friend."

"Good," John said. "I don't need no Irish troubles."

I'd been nursing the Guinness, but I had no intention of finishing it. I didn't drink before noon. Alcoholics did that. Some writers like my friend Dick did that. John did have a legitimate problem here. I asked John when the Costigan brothers last announced themselves.

"Yesterday."

Neither Jimmy nor Malcolm told me when they had last seen Boo. It was sloppy police work on my part not to have established a timeline. The question that stopped the traffic in my head was how Mr. B would act, because the man didn't tolerate disrespect, and whoever disrupted the cash flow to him wouldn't find himself in the good hands of Allstate Insurance.

"Change of subject now," I said, "What can you tell me about Izzy Duncan?"

John's eyebrows fussed, and he hooted, "Who?" like an owl.

"Some kid Bonnie asked me to look into. Lives in your neck of the woods."

"Lives in Dorchester, huh."

"Yeah."

"You think all black people know each other?"

"He lives in your neighborhood, so I thought I'd ask."

"Think we all look alike, too?"

"Thought we all bleed red?"

"Not according to massah."

John refused my money for the beer. He pushed it away. I reminded him that I'd talk to our mutual friend.

"Thanks, and say hi to Bonnie for me and tell her I said she could do better."

I walked out of the bar into the bright sunlight of Mass Ave. Horns honked. An anonymous voice shouted an expletive and insulted someone's mother. These Costigan brothers were putting the Irish squeeze on John, on Mr. B, and Jimmy. The last thing Boston needed was a Civil War, the North End versus Southie.

Chapter Six: Deliveries

It was noon when I got to the intersection of State and Washington at the bottom of the Financial District. I ignored the hideous Government Center to admire the Ames on Court Street. The Ames was Boston's first skyscraper and an example of Romanesque Revival architecture in Milford granite and Ohio sandstone. It was the tall city kid among Boston buildings until the Federal bullies redid the Custom House, and then came the Prudential Tower. I was determined to reach Bonnie's office on State Street before the offices unleashed hordes of lunchtime barbarians.

Brand new building, brand new skyscraper, a titan of pink granite, she stared down at government buildings and offered an emperor's view of the city, including the Charles and Mystic Rivers. I walked against the tide of pedestrians. Around me, bankers and lawyers, office drones and secretaries brushed past me. And when the light changed, cars honked and advanced one city-inch at a time. Out of the hundreds of offices came thousands of hungry faces. I swam towards a faux-gold door handle to access the lobby. Inside this vestibule of bright lights and brighter marble, city sounds vanished. An elevator chimed, and two people exited. A guard sat behind a desk. Out of view, his hands could reach for a phone, a clipboard, or whatever it took to pacify visitors.

I gave him Bonnie's name and floor number. He dialed a number and expressed the pertinent information as if I were the family's shame there for a visit. The law firm—and I expected no less from blue bloods—was on the thirty-eighth floor. I was told to wait a moment.

"Jesus, Mary, and Joseph. Is that you, Cleary?"

Another guard, back from his break, appeared. He presented himself in a starched uniform, the nickel-plated star above his left breast pocket, but I didn't need to see a nameplate on the right to recognize him. My heart sank. Lobby security guard was apparently where old Boston cops went to die.

"Halloran?"

"One and the same. I'm impressed you remembered me. It's been a long time."

He pumped my hand in a vigorous handshake. Halloran was old guard when I'd been a rookie. Good cop, bad divorce. He fell back on Security to generate income since the ex was bleeding him dry for support. She lived the high life on his dime, and she played Mrs. Robinson to every young buck within the zip code while he pulled long hours to foot her lifestyle. She dropped her fling du jour when he thought matrimony because marriage would stop the free ride. She read prospects for the bedroom faster than Fagin and his band of pickpockets. We talked. I listened to a decade's worth of misery and gossip compressed into a series of half sentences, shrugs, and sighs until I heard the elevator's bell ring.

A pair of heels clicked their way to me. My eyes appreciated the fine figure of an office girl in a mannish coat, Faye Dunaway floppy hat, and an accordion folder pressed against her chest.

"Mr. Cleary, I presume?"

"At your service. And you are?"

She said her name without relaxing her hold on the goods pressed against her. I held out my hand, and she looked at it, puzzled. She handed the parcel to me with a hesitant smile. I undid the elastic band to have a peek inside. Judging from the amount of paperwork, there was enough there to turn a case of stolen jewelry into a long stretch in Walpole for the sap who had a Public Defender for a lawyer. I snapped the elastic back and tucked the file folder under my arm.

She was still standing there. She would have done well in the military. The lawyers upstairs didn't appreciate her diligence, her seeing matters through. To them, she was the help, another girl from the South Shore.

"How long have you been working for the firm, Siobhán?

34

Her eyes widened. "Six months. I'm a legal assistant."

"Why did you look so surprised that I asked a question?"

"You're the first person to pronounce my name correctly."

"May I offer you some unsolicited advice, Siobhán?"

"Sure."

"You're a legal assistant, which means the bosses on the farm upstairs bill for your time, though they treat you like a secretary. You deserve more respect." I reached into my jacket and took out my wallet. I handed her a card. "There's the name of a professor I know on the card. Tell him I sent you. Talk to him. If you're interested in taking the LSAT, he's your man."

"I already work for one of the top-shelf law firms in Boston, Mr. Cleary."

"Shane," I said. "Be more than the Irish help, or not. Your choice." I pointed to the card. "He'll know how to pronounce your name."

I returned to the lobby desk and asked Halloran to dial the firm's number for me. After he handed the receiver to me, I asked the secretary on the line to patch me through to Bonnie.

Bonnie recognized my voice and said, "Get the package?"

"I did. Not to sound impertinent, Bonnie, but bring the paperwork down yourself next time."

"I'm busy." Her voice was sharp, but I had her attention. "What's wrong?"

"I'm not the help. Pro bono, remember?"

I walked over to Court Square to a favorite sandwich place close to Pi Alley. Ordered myself two pastrami sandwiches with the works. Extra kosher pickles. I checked the sky. Boston was home to birds. Peregrine falcons nested inside the Custom House. Pigeons were everywhere, but I spotted a raven. Ravens spooked me as a kid after I read Carlo Collodi's novel *Pinocchio* thinking I'd get the Disney film's version and didn't.

A customer behind me tapped my shoulder, and I accepted my sandwiches.

Back on Washington Street, a familiar lamppost doubled as a timepiece outside my office building. Sean at the front desk nodded hello. My first stop was at the jeweler's on the ground floor to find Saul Fiedermann. I handed him a pastrami sandwich with extra pickles.

"There's no such thing as a free lunch," he said.

"Consider it an advance on a favor?"

"What favor?"

"You'll find out. Enjoy your lunch, Saul."

He peeked inside the bag. "This isn't good for my heart, for my blood pressure. My wife would be very upset if she found out."

"Only if she finds out, Saul. Only if she finds out."

In the lobby, I pressed the button for the seventh floor and my office. Some days the hallways and offices ran cold, other days the iron radiators hissed enough steam to take out the wrinkles in your shirt and the lines in your face. The doors opened, and I started the walk to my office.

The Province building was to step into another era. It was easy to think of Prohibition: dice games and midday assignations that included a nip of gin and some quick sex where neither party complained about the duration or quality. Henry Miller and Anaïs Nin or Henry James and whoever would have been happy here, in any one of the rooms.

I unlocked my door, picked the mail up off the floor, and then acted like the governor with requests. I decided who would receive clemency and who would die in the metal trashcan. I undid the elastic snap and removed the paperwork Siobhán undoubtedly organized for me at Bonnie's request. I also removed my lunch, which received the proper reverence. The sandwich's wrapper was laid out with an Egyptologist's respect for a map of the Valley of the Kings. And with that taste of smoked and salty goodness between two slices of rye bread with caramelized onions and mustard, I flew close to the sun.

After lunch, I thumbed through the rest of the file on Israel Duncan.

Dorchester kid.

Beacon Hill robbery.

I wanted to locate the details around the B&E to find the open window somewhere in the reports. As a former cop and practitioner of the prose style that eschewed adverbs as ornamental and adjectives as judgmental, I had to find that mote of dust, that speck of a detail. Cops write for the broadest audience and the pickiest of critics: the lawyers with red pens and the judge with a blue pencil. The final audience was the jurors in the box.

Izzy scowled in his mug shot. Perception started there. Intake at the station house treated suspects like cattle. Poke. Prod. Move them along. Answer the wrong way, with the wrong tone, and it earned the collared guests a twist of the cuffs or a hard bump against the bars. Accidents happened, too. Suspects have fallen down a flight of stairs headfirst. A remarkable accomplishment when leg irons were used. The easiest tactic was to claim overcrowding and place the fresh meat with the hardened crowd in the lockup.

Izzy's foray into the criminal life started off on the wrong note. Pinched after he'd stolen a pair of earrings for his mother at the Five and Dime, the charge shouldn't have stuck, but he was black, and he made the mistake of mouthing off to a correctional officer. The screws added another charge to his sheet while he was in Holding. Rather than put the kid in a live episode from the Scared Straight program, the judge packed him off to Cottage 9 in Shirley. No small miracle Izzy hadn't come out of that particular hellhole a psychopath. Even cops hated returning runaways to the facility. The stories were awful: fingers broken for the smallest infraction; solitary confinement was a room with no windows or toilet; floors were scrubbed clean with the only toothbrush an inmate owned; and the sexual crimes would make you cross yourself even if you weren't Catholic. Israel Duncan had survived all that. Years later, at twenty-one years old, life dealt him another card from the bottom of the deck. Page after page of statements placed Izzy in the vicinity. Purely circumstantial, but factor in the color of skin, his prior brush with the law, and Izzy looked good for it.

Charles Armstrong claimed that a black male had broken into his residence and stole his wife's sapphire and diamond engagement ring. The stolen item was a family heirloom. Victorian. The file included a picture from the insurance company, along with an appraisal. The gems were classified as violet-blue sapphires, over five carats, in coronet settings. Two cushion-cut diamonds that weighed in at a touch over two carats were part of the setting. I didn't care for the gold mounting. The appraiser valued granny's bauble at a hundred grand.

Izzy protested his innocence. The cops turned his place inside out.

Nothing.

Izzy accounted for his presence in the neighborhood, saying that he'd cut through Beacon Hill on his way to Mass General to visit his sick aunt. He worked in a bistro kitchen in Back Bay and said the walk from the job to the hospital cleared his mind and saved him some money from using public transportation. His employer and the nurses supported the story.

I stopped reading and closed the jacket.

A professional thief improves on his or her craft. Izzy's first arrest was as childish as kindergarten. There's a world of difference between poaching a pair of dime store earrings and an expensive ring, between shoplifting and felony theft. Whoever stole it understood the ring's value and the address where it lived. The police report didn't mention any other items stolen inside the Armstrong residence, but photographs documented how the thief hacked at the lock on the door like a Civil War field surgeon amputated a leg.

The DA would have jurors believe that Izzy was a sophisticated cat burglar, a black version of Cary Grant in *To Catch a Thief*, dancing from one rooftop to the next. Lady Justice is blind, but she isn't stupid. Beacon Hill wasn't the French Riviera, and those twelve members of the jury weren't his peers.

I had an idea. I put everything away except for one item.

I went downstairs for a word with Saul. I put the photograph on the glass case in front of him.

"Handsome ring," he said. I asked him for his opinion. He wiped his hands on a napkin before he examined the glossy photo. Saul was an expert. He didn't need the lingerie description. He could guess the carat weight for each sapphire and diamond by looking at the picture. He could narrow down the names of the studio and the craftsman in the last century responsible for the mounting. His eyes were that perceptive and knowledgeable. He placed the photo down on the counter.

"How do I pay for my lunch?" he said.

"Put the word out that you have a client interested in a ring like that."

"And?"

"And your client values discretion above all."

"And," he repeated.

"Call me if something pops up."

"In other words, a fence or a collector."

"I'm not choosy," I said. I wasn't.

Saul picked up the photo. He sighed. "It was a good sandwich."

Chapter Seven: In Play

Sean at the front desk put a hiccup in my exit. He handed me a sealed envelope and apologized for not having given me the message earlier. Sean said that the overnight concierge left it behind, and he had not seen it. I told Sean not to worry about it. We chatted. He recommended a film noir retrospective of all three versions of *The Maltese Falcon* playing at Coolidge Corner.

I ran a finger through the seal to open the impromptu mail from Bill, my buddy who worked the city's tenderloin district and underbelly undercover, whether it was the Combat Zone or high-end escort agencies for the BPD. The cops in Vice joked that women were entering law schools in record numbers, so tuition had to get paid somehow.

Bill was good at his job because he was clean-cut, good-looking, and didn't sport the edge that most seasoned cops carried with them, which was worth a laugh because Bill, like me, was a Vietnam vet. We'd both seen and done things no young kid should have.

A great cop. Bill was—how should we say it—a man who preferred the company of other men. That fact mattered little to me, but discretion was paramount to Bill's career. Cops talk about brotherhood, but they might be slow to cover someone's back if he were queer. This was Boston, a town founded by Puritans who equated a sneeze with an orgasm, and most of its cops were Irish and Catholic. Bill was that living contradiction between public and private, wrapped in mothballs and tucked deep inside a closet. The women libbers said the personal was political, and political was personal, but they'd never been in the dark waiting for backup. I couldn't care less how he fluffed the pillows or for whom because, to me, he was a brother in arms and, as I'd said, an honest and reliable cop.

Bill had written a first and last name on the slip inside the envelope. Nothing else.

Perhaps he thought the P in PI stood for psychic. I ripped up the piece of paper and envelope and tossed the shreds into one of the few trash barrels on Washington Street. I'd get the relevant details later. I'd let him sleep the day off like a vampire. I, on the other hand, had to visit Mr. B in the North End.

I raised my hands for the frisk from Mr. B's bodyguard. Tony Two-Times stood nearby, masticating a wad of Big Red gum and reeked of cinnamon.

"Back to trying to quit smoking again, Tony?"

"Tried trying."

"I hear quitting smokes is harder than shaking heroin."

"You implying I'm a junkie or something?"

"Not at all, Tony. The something is called compassion."

"Keep it to yourself, Cleary, and about that thing we discussed, remember?"

"Yeah, I do, and I suggested that you call my answering service with a date and time."

"Change of plans," he said as security finished the pat-down.

"What change of plans?"

"When you're done with the boss, I want you to go down to Vittoria and wait for me. We'll go from there."

"Today?"

"Got a date lined up today, or what?"

"It's a bit sudden, don't you think, Tony?"

"Learn to be spontaneous, Cleary. Spontaneity keeps you young and alive."

"Alive is the operative word. I'll see you at Vittoria. Will I have time to enjoy a pastry?"

"Enjoy whatever you want. It's a free country. Now, follow me."

I followed Tony to a backroom to meet with his boss.

Mr. B was first generation Cosa Nostra after Luciano formed the

Commission. Booze, bets, and broads had been his bread and butter as a young hood. He agreed with the Board's policy to steer clear of narcotics. The way I understood it, the Committee couldn't dictate to bosses, but they offered advice, whereas bosses determined policy.

Mr. B perceived narcotics as something artists and musicians did for inspiration or to keep their fantasy world turning round on the carousel. Whether it was weed or other forms of dope, Mr. B disliked nature's pharmacy. The objection to narcotics was that they could and would find their way onto school playgrounds. Mr. B argued kids were kids, and adults chose to drink, gamble, and whore. Times changed, and he was in the minority. Profits screamed louder than any kids in the schoolyard.

Tony led the way to a backroom. This long stroll was intended to discourage a hitter. He'd have to work hard to hit his mark and then work harder to survive the egress. The air smelled of garlic and lemons. Italian restaurants had a thing for dim and dimmer lighting. Small red candles with white netting lit the procession route until I found Mr. B on a curved leather sectional, sitting and sipping a glass of red wine. He told Tony he could leave and I could sit.

"To what do I owe the pleasure, Mr. Cleary?"

"Working a case and a question surfaced."

A waiter buzzed in, and Mr. B asked whether I wanted something to eat or drink. I mentioned the pastrami sandwich for lunch. Mr. B insisted that I have a glass of sparkling water. Aided digestion, he commented. The waiter disappeared and reappeared with the effervescent beverage with a lemon twist.

"I don't want to pry," I said, "but I'd like to know whether there are any Irish problems I should know about?"

My question amused him. "More like when don't I have a problem with your people."

"With all due respect, they're not my people. Every group has their share of idiots."

"What seems to be the problem?"

"Our friend who owns a bar received the shake-down. He was under the impression that he shouldn't have that problem."

"Why didn't he come to me?"

I let my hand do the grand sweep to indicate the room. "When was the last time a black man entered this room?"

"I'll have someone look into it."

"Please do, because I think he's a little confused."

"Confused about what?"

"Having to pay protection twice."

Mr. B might've had seventy-something-year-old eyes, but he had 80-proof venom in his veins. He raised a hand, and Tony manifested tableside.

"Mr. Cleary says his friend in Central Square has had a run-in with some Irish hooligans. Remember him?"

"The shine?"

"Jesus, Tony. Show some sensitivity, will ya?" Mr. B said with some exasperation.

Tony stood there, dense and thick as a human refrigerator. "What?"

"Remember the Civil Rights Movement?"

"Yeah, and tell me, what's changed?"

"Never mind. See what you can find out."

Tony looked to me and jutted his chin. "Have anything that could save me some time?"

"Southie. Two guys, possibly brothers."

Tony didn't say a word. He walked away, leaving me alone with his boss. I didn't give the name Costigan because I wanted Tony to work for the score in case either John had the name wrong or Malcolm did. If it were the Costigans giving John the Irish squeeze, they might get off with some love from Tony and the disciplinary committee. If they'd stolen Jimmy's dog, they were as good as dead.

Mr. B touched my wrist. "You think these guys work for Jimmy?"

"Maybe, maybe not."

"Independents?" Mr. B looked at me, serious. "You were seconds away from becoming an anchovy inside a tin can because of Jimmy. I'm Catholic, like you, and I can forgive, but that doesn't mean I forget."

Jimmy and his handler had me and Mr. B's nephew trussed up inside a car, inside a compactor. Jimmy and his friend left while we were on our way to becoming a small cube of compressed metal, flesh, and bone.

I thanked him for his time, for his help, and for the drink, which I knocked back. The fizz scorched the roof off my palate. Helping John out was in play. I needed to find out what Bill wanted done with the name in his message to me. I'd have to put that into play, too, and I might have time to get myself back to finding Boo, the missing dog.

Maybe. Maybe not.

Chapter Eight: The Other Side

The bolt of espresso was halfway to my stomach when Tony said we had to leave Caffé Vittoria *pronto*. I had arrived minutes ago, ordered coffee and a pastry when Tony opened the door and made his announcement. Hat on his lid, gun holstered, and overcoat on, Tony resembled Dick Butkus for size, speed, and ferocity. In and out the front door with an order to move fast, I left as a server pulled a lever, and the massive espresso machine screamed steam. I was forced to inhale my cannoli and hit Hanover Street with powdered sugar still on my lips.

He threw the bolt and locked my door as I hopped into the passenger seat. I'd wanted to ask him why the accent ran the wrong way on the sign for the café, but Tony was all grunts and grumbles. For the word coffee, the Italian dictionary said *caffè* and not *caffé*, and I wondered if the sign-maker had made a mistake.

Inside the vehicle, there was no hello, no nothing, only the sounds of the Cadillac's engine and the radio on low. We sat there for a few seconds before I heard, "Off to the Lake as promised. Put on your seatbelt."

I glanced over the wrong shoulder. Tony noticed and said, "Seat buckle is on the other side."

"I was looking to see if there was a friend in the backseat."

"If I was going to clip you, you think I would use my own car?" His voice conveyed a mood somewhere between misery and the edge of menace. "Suppose you believe in cement shoes and one last smoke on a long pier before the big drink."

I shifted in my seat. "No, Tony, I don't, and you know why?"

His eyes dug into my face. "Why?"

"The preferred method these days is an oil drum. Johnny Roselli, for example. He was found inside of one, in some bay north of Miami."

"Handsome Johnny was with The Outfit in Chicago. This is Boston."

"Why waste a good harbor? If you don't drown, the pollution kills you." I waved a finger. "And one minor correction, my friend. The late Mr. Roselli lived his formative years right here in Boston. Now, can we get this show on the road? I've got things to do."

"Like what?"

"Working a case."

"How could I forget? You're in search of Fifi the Poodle."

Tony shifted the behemoth of a car from park to drive. He drove, and I people-watched. New Englanders on sidewalks trudged to their nine-to-five, accepting the possibility of all five types of weather in one day, unlike their predecessors, the Puritans, who saw darkness everywhere they went. They tamed the wilderness as if it were a garden, and the Indians were weeds. Those Calvinist men with the buckle hats and funny collars were less tolerant of those who disagreed with them on matters of faith, grace, and predestination. Their descendants felt the same way about the Yankees, the Bruins, the Celtics, and the Red Sox.

We floated through city streets. In the swirl of thoughts and images, with people as postcards outside my window, I reconsidered the word 'wilderness' from another religious angle, as in T.S. Eliot's poem and his phrase, 'wilderness of mirrors,' which has come to be associated with the treachery and spy novels about the Cold War, but I disagreed with Tom, the poet. The echo inside my head while Tony drove was more mimetic, more real, and more dangerous. When Eliot had penned the phrase, he was describing the ramblings of an old man in "Gerontion."

Tony Two-Times was unlikely to reach old age, unlikely to receive the AARP card in the mail and pop Geritol for vitamins until he dropped. I doubt he'd contemplate peaches and the passage of time as he gamboled along the strand of Revere Beach, his pant legs rolled up like J. Alfred Prufrock. No, not Tony Two-Times. He lived the hard and fast, short and dangerous life, where the majority of men in his line of work retired with lead poisoning or lengthy prison sentences. Roselli was a prime example. Roselli was Hollywood handsome, and he caroused and partied with starlets. Despite the glamour and intrigue of spooks around him and all those innuendos that he'd been party to a presidential assassination, Johnny did not live to be old and gray, nor did his boss in Chicago, also called to testify about his role in killing Boston's favorite son. No, packed inside an oil drum was not what most people thought of when they heard 'burial at sea.'

There were more sidewalks and more people, and I realized we weren't headed to the Pike for the cruise control to the Lake, to Nonatum, to Tony's village near Newton. At around the time I'd come to my senses and oriented myself, Tony made the captain's announcement.

"There's been a change of plans."

I said nothing. I watched Tony chomp on a wad of chewing gum in his latest attempt at breaking the nicotine habit. I asked for a piece, and he gave me one. While I chewed, he seemed interested in what I was doing with the sliver of aluminum that Wrigley wrapped around their gum. I answered before he asked.

"When I was a kid, my friends and I believed that if you could peel the wax paper from the foil, your wish came true."

"Yeah? What's your wish today? Wait, asking is the jinx."

"I'll tell you anyway," I said. "I wish I knew where I was going."

"I gotta thing I need to take care of first."

"A thing?"

"Yeah, a thing, and it needs to be taken care of first."

"Is this thing related to the thing I asked you to look into?"

"What's it to you?" he said.

"I don't know what worries me more, Tony. This 'thing,' or what 'taken care of' means."

That made Tony smile as we coasted into a parking spot. As I lifted myself out of the leather interior of his Cadillac, some kid for a valet rushed us. He was in the last sprint of his sentence, saying, "Hey! You retards can't park," but swallowed the last word when he saw Tony rise to full height on the driver's side.

I read the sign: THE OTHER SIDE.

We were in Bay Village. I'd heard of the place from Bill and the other Jimmy in my life, also gay, but an arsonist instead of the gangster from Southie. Tony brought the kid to heel. "What's with you, kid?"

The kid sputtered some nonsense. I was worried he'd have an accident in his pants.

Tony didn't let up. "Why aren't you in school?"

"I'm not so good at it, and my family needs the money."

Tony pointed to the sign. "And here is where you make your bread?"

"Money is money."

Tony parted the front of his jacket and reached into his pocket. The teen looked as if he'd have a coronary and expected the white light at the end of the tunnel and the sound of God's voice. Tony said, "Relax, will ya? Here." Tony handed him a crisp twenty. "Watch the car for me, and here is the key, in case you have to move it. You can handle a Cadillac, right?"

"Think so."

"Word of advice, kid. Speak with confidence. Don't say, 'I think.' Say, 'I can, or yes."

"I can. I mean, yes," the kid responded.

"And another thing, don't use the word 'retard.' It's demeaning."

Tony and I walked into the joint, a staple in the hunger for gay entertainment in the Village. There were other places in this part of town. On the scale from tame to decadence worthy of Caligula, Bay Village ran the range from the genteel piano-bar crowd of Napoleon's to the middle of the road of Jacque's for the after-the-theatre audience to The Punch Bowl, which required vitamins, shots of penicillin and B-12, chased with a rigorous regimen of hydration after the debauchery.

I passed a billboard on a tripod. The main act was a drag queen named Silvia Sidney, who performed with headdresses that would've made Carmen Miranda jealous. Sidney's most outré costume included a necklace made from toilet seats. The stage name came from a movie actress from the Golden Age of Hollywood, and like that actress Silvia Sidney from Roxbury had been born Jewish, the youngest of eight kids.

Tony said a name at the counter, and the bar-back pointed to an office in the back of the house. Tony looked to me and said, "You can come or stay, your choice."

"I'll come, but I don't want to be a part of any rough stuff."

"Afraid you'll break a nail? Relax, Cleary, and follow me."

The place was silent, the air dead. In this back office sat a balding guy, who finessed the few strands of hair left on his dome into a ridiculous combover. If they were the spaghetti for the two dogs in "Lady and the Tramp," those two dogs would've died from want of love and nutrition.

I stood stone silent and listened to the subtitles while Tony informed the manager that he had heard that he, the illustrious overseer of this fine establishment, had 'shorted a friend' of his. Whether stupidity ran in his family or he possessed the gonads of Zeus himself, this guy mouthed off to Tony. He was quick to employ the Anglo-Saxon side of the English language. I didn't catch everything he said, but the guy ranted about freaks, queers, weirdos, transvestites, and trannies. Tony listened to the diatribe and said nothing.

"Are you done?" Tony asked him.

"Yeah, I'm done. Now get the f—"

Tony interrupted him mid-sentence, like he did with the parking valet, except this didn't come with advice or a sharp Andrew Jackson. Tony snatched the guy by the throat, lifted him up, and kept him suspended in mid-air. While he writhed, Tony talked.

"Listen to me, wannabe tough guy. He's a friend of mine. He does his job, and I expect him to get paid for services rendered."

Tony dropped the guy. On all fours, on the floor, coughing, he gasped, "I don't get it."

"What's there to get? He works. You pay. What's to understand?"

"He's a nobody. What concern is it of yours?"

"Like I said, he's a friend."

"You're friends with a drag queen?"

"It's a job. He's an entertainer. Have you looked at your clientele most nights?"

The manager stood up. The light overhead highlighted the slick of sweat and oil, or both, on his bald head. He dared to justify himself. "I take a cut. Anyone who works here kicks a percentage from their tips to me. It's the privilege of working The Other Side. You, of all people, should know how it works."

"Then change the policy or make an exception," Tony said. When he parted his jacket again, I worried. Tony took a step forward. "And another thing, don't disrespect your employees the way you do."

"What the hell you talking about?"

"You called them degenerates, freaks, and faggots."

The guy looked genuinely shocked. "But your friend is queer, a drag queen."

All six-six of Tony looked as if he were ready to drill the guy into the floorboards.

"Let me enlighten you. The man you called a faggot and a degenerate isn't any of those things."

The man held up both hands. "He's your friend. I get it. I get it."

"No, I don't think you do. He's a teacher. History and music are his subjects. He works this sewer because he needs the money. He has a lovely wife, and his kid has special needs, but the three jobs between the two of them don't cover the bills for their kid. You follow?" The runt nodded while Tony laid into him some more. "That summers-off crap people seem to think is "The Life of Riley" of teachers isn't. Rob him, and you steal from me. The next thing I want to hear is that you restored him."

"'Restored him'? What the hell does that mean?"

"As in, you made him whole again, paid him what you stole from him, and I'd appreciate if you kicked in extra for the inconvenience. If I hear otherwise, that sign over the door that says The Other Side will have another meaning for you. Are we clear?"

After a quick drop off of something from Tony's trunk to another friend in Waltham, we took the scenic route through Auburndale, a quaint burb along the Charles River. Tony gave me the docent's tour. He mentioned the amusement park, which had died around the same time my father did. Tony said that was a good thing because zoos made him sad. Bad people deserved to be behind bars, not beautiful creatures meant to live wild. He said the idea of animals on display bothered him.

On our ride, he told me that the Norumbega Park had once housed a zoo, and nearby Newton-Wellesley Hospital opened a special unit within its Emergency Room because animals went AWOL from the zoo. Monkeys were notorious for biting people.

As we drifted through the hamlet, Tony pointed out other highlights, such as the Totem Pole Ballroom, where his mother danced during the Depression, to the boathouse, which acted as a station for the Metropolitan Police. We drove past the Knotty Pine, a diner-slash-luncheonette, where the locals gathered for coffee, conversation, and argued over sports.

We stopped at a makeshift sign that said Ken's Flower Café. There was no coffee or any food served there, but plenty of flowers that a guy—whom I presumed was Kenny—sold out of a VW bug. Tony left me in the car like I was the family pet. When he returned, he was armed with two arrangements of long-stemmed roses, each one wrapped with enough waxed paper and cellophane that I couldn't see his face. One bouquet was red roses with baby's breath, the other, without the breath. He placed the flowers on the backseat.

"One is for Bonnie," he said.

"Which one?"

"The one without baby's breath."

"Why doesn't she get one with baby's breath?"

"What's wrong with you?" Tony cold-eyed me. "Baby's breath is bad for Delilah. Don't you know that?"

"Apparently not. I didn't know you liked Delilah."

"I like pets. Like kids, too, until they're older and become the animals I don't like." He glared at me. "Learn something today, and hear what I have to say because it concerns Delilah."

"You're not exactly what comes to mind for Marlin Perkins and Mutual of Omaha's Wild Kingdom."

"Good, because it ain't Sunday night either. Now, pay attention, for

51

Delilah's sake. No fir or spruce tree for Christmas decorations, and forget pine. All of them are dangerous to her, and don't forget those holiday flowers, which means no amaryllis, holly and mistletoe, and no poinsettias. Oh, and no Easter lilies either."

"You're a horticultural wonder, Tony, you know that?"

"You think you're funny, don't you, Cleary?"

"I try."

"I wish you wouldn't." He pulled the car out of park but kept his foot on the brake. "This poor guy here, in front of us. He works this stand every day of the year except New Year's. I asked him why he doesn't get a roof over his head, and he told me the city's zoning laws forbid it. Makes no sense. This guy ain't taking from anyone, unlike that jerk in town, and he can't catch a break. Makes zero sense to me. He sells happiness, and that other mook terrorizes his people."

We did the K-turn. Nobody anywhere, and Tony was as cautious, law-abiding, and proper a driver as Dudley Do-Right. He enumerated the rules of the homestead when we'd arrived and parked in front of his mother's house. Her name was Carmen, but I was not to speak to her unless she spoke to me. I listened to his dissertation on Sicilian etiquette, and at one point, I had to stop him.

"I can't keep up. First, you tell me you want a Latin tutor for your niece, but it can't be a man because your niece is living inside some Regency romance novel, and—"

"What are you saying, Cleary?"

"Why am I here? Bonnie should be here, not me."

"We talked about this."

"No, what we talked about is not having a direct connection between your pocket and Bonnie's purse. As you so eloquently explained to me, Bonnie has to appear spotless because of the Bar Association. That's what we discussed, Tony."

"And my mother is paying you, not Bonnie." He stared at me, expression-less.

Another blank stare, my own. There was a gap in comprehension, on both sides of the leather armrest, large enough that I heard the iceberg that sank the Titanic yawn. I had nothing and repeated my wearied question. "Why is she paying me when paying her establishes no connection between you and Bonnie?"

"Because you're the man."

I looked to the radio, at the visor, before they confronted Tony's. Unbelievable.

"I give up." I threw my hands up in despair.

"My mother believes any money coming into a house belongs to the man."

"You did explain to your mother that Bonnie is her own woman, didn't you?"

"It don't matter."

"She's a lawyer, Tony."

He shook his head. "Makes no difference to her."

"As for house, it's Bonnie's place."

He was agitated. "My mother don't need to know the two of you are living in sin."

"'Living in sin'? You're serious."

"I have a sense of humor, but not when it comes to my mother. None of us do."

Tony had thrown gears on me, so I asked, "Who is us?"

"The guys on the street. Guys like me. Let me explain something to you, Cleary. Every one of us has a mother, but nobody has a mother like a Sicilian." He looked both ways as if he was worried someone had overheard him. "You know me and Mr. B. We're not afraid of nobody. Guys on the street, they know there are rules and there are consequences. You get called for when you break a rule, and there's a good chance you walk into a sit-down, and you don't walk out. You follow?"

"Like I am in a dark room. Make your point, Tony."

"My point is there are rules, like I said, but when it comes to Sicilian mothers, you never know what to expect. They have this way. I don't know how to explain it."

"Try, Tony. I'm sitting right here."

"They have a way of getting under your skin. Nothing you do is right. Ever. Everything you do is either wrong or it coulda been done better. God help you when they throw you a compliment. Those require an act of Congress, and you know it's a set-up."

"Same could be said about Jewish mothers."

"No, this is different. It's all a matter of style, how they stick it to you. It's never a criticism, but a suggestion. It's never an insult; it's an observation. It's always done clean and fast, like an ice pick. I oughta know."

Tony pulled aside his shirt collar. I saw the scar.

Rather than say 'mommy issues,' I conceded defeat. "I forgot. Machiavelli was a broad."

I asked him what the history was between him and the teacher who worked at The Other Side. He told me that the teacher had helped his father after he had had a stroke. A doctor clued Tony in on singing as a way for his old man to recover from his medical calamity.

The music-slash-history teacher had taught Tony's father how to sing. He said they started with the Julie Andrews song "Do-Re-Mi" from *The Sound of Music*. The vocal exercises retrained the muscles and rewired the part of the brain affected by the stroke. Tony said his old man made a decent enough recovery that he regained most of his speech after a long, laborious regimen of unorthodox therapy.

"The irony of ironies," Tony said, "is that I didn't know the guy's money went in one hand and into another one because of his kid's expenses." I could see wetness in Tony's eyes. "My old man is dead, but I will tell you this. My father didn't die shriveled up into some shell of his former self, thanks to that teacher. I didn't go broke either. You have any idea how much nursing homes cost? People say we're bad, but those homes for old folks have nothing on us; they're the real crooks. So much for The Great Society LBJ promised. Anyhow, those exercises restored some decency and dignity to my old man. Understand?"

"Yeah, I do. He made him whole."

We had arrived, and he parked the car.

"Damn straight. Now, let's get this over with. Ma would kill this pity party.

54

I don't expect you to understand her, Cleary. Maybe it's a Mediterranean thing, a Sicilian thing, and it's different with you Irish, but this is our way. Humor me and let's chalk this up to she wants to meet you."

"Okay, I'm the man of the house, but set me straight on something here, Tony."

Armed with flowers, we stood there in the street. "What now? The neighbors are watching us."

"When we first talked about your niece, you said you needed to ask your mother for permission. Is it because your sister and niece live in her house?"

"That's half of it." Tony looked embarrassed, and it was the first time in all the time I'd known him he couldn't look at me. He took a breath. "She is old-school, meaning she's particular about who she lets into her house. Emphasis here is her house."

He looked at me while I did the mental calculations. "This is because I'm Irish?"

"Because you're Irish."

I shook my head in disbelief. "Anyone else she's particular about?"

Tony didn't hesitate. "Take your pick. Blacks. Jews. Where do we start?"

"Question isn't where we start, Tony. It's where does it end?"

I climbed the steps into the homestead, into another world of aromas, of food on the stove, cooking for hours on end. I conceded to the generational and cultural divide between Sicilian and Hibernian, but Tony didn't understand that Irish mothers were no different. Only their methods varied. For any harm that befell her child, an Irish mother would sit in a folding chair in torrential rain, smoke her cig to the quick and kill you just the same or wait for you in Hell if she missed you.

While Tony called out to her, I waited where I stood. I ignored the plastic on the furniture, the room in mustard yellow that would've sent van Gogh screaming into the wheat fields. I ignored the desiccated palm frond on the wall, and I ignored the crucifix, the tray of rosary beads, and the ball of scapular necklaces that Delilah would've mistaken for yarn.

I saw the silhouette. I could not ignore the cliché of a diminutive woman and her giant for a son. He said something in dialect and handed her the bushel of roses. I witnessed the passive-aggressive fuss from *materfamilias*, such as 'You shouldn't have' and 'You're throwing money away on something that will die soon.'

My eyes couldn't look away from her ironing board.

The woman ironed her son's money.

Chapter Nine: Up Here

A new morning, a fresh start, and I decided to retrace the trail that put Israel Duncan in jail.

I started behind Beacon Hill, that place I thought of as the backyard of the State House. The Hill was where the career politicians ruled this town from their offices with dark wood and ugly portraits of their predecessors on the walls. When power wasn't in session, they'd steal away to their clubs for drinks at the wooden bar and counter or prolonged lunches inside reserved booths. Whether it was over Scotches or martinis, the pols decided fates, brokered deals, and ended their visits with a trip to the washroom where there were long troughs filled with chipped ice for a urinal, the stalls with toilets and pull-chains and water tanks overhead.

The Chinese laundry was new, and the all-night coffee shop offered a pit stop for the Suffolk Law students. The movie *The Paper Chase* had hoodwinked them into a life of paper cuts and silverfish in the library. Suffolk wasn't Calvinist Harvard, but it wasn't Catholic BC either. A Mainer named Gleason Archer founded the school in gratitude to George Frost, who had loaned him the money for his legal education and secured him a position at a law firm. When Frost refused payment, Archer honored his benefactor by teaching law in the parlor of his home in Roxbury before his "Archer's Evening Law School" became the law school on the Hill.

Bonnie was an alumna of Suffolk, and I walked the grounds she covered as a student. Progressive as it seemed to allow women into the legal profession, allowing a black kid like Israel Duncan to walk through sacred Brahmin space seemed liberal, but it wasn't.

Israel Duncan could walk wherever he pleased, so long as he kept on walking. He'd summit the steep hill, mill around the State House's gold dome, and then descend another hill to Cambridge Street on his way to Mass General Hospital.

Cambridge Street was where democracy and the rabble mixed together. Down, there were liquor stores, second-tier bars, and cheap flats for families of patients. There was also the Charles River. Up in the tall buildings, the river looked like a dark ribbon, and it provided a view of other offices and the brownstones etched into Beacon Hill. There were a number of streets that bled into Cambridge Street that the kid could have taken for his trips to see his beloved aunt in MGH.

I was more interested in Duncan's arc of ascent and descent because the victims, Mr. and Mrs. Armstrong, lived not far from the hospital. Bonnie's paperwork stated the cops had detected no scent of booze on the suspect. This ruled out their conducting any interviews at any number of the bars and pubs that dotted Cambridge Street. Bonnie's file on Duncan's arrest also included photographs of the jimmied door and lock. A blind man in a barbershop could have done a better job at a B&E.

The nurses said that he was never late visiting his aunt. They stated in the documentation that, on the day of the robbery and arrest, he didn't look tired or distressed. His boss and another coworker established when he had left the job. The timeline into town, for the robbery itself, and then at his aunt's bedside was tight.

Too tight.

In my experience, thieves cased the scene. Pros knew every detail about their score. They'd know when traffic lights changed, whether the buses ran on schedule, and who walked his dog when and where. The last thing a burglar wanted were eyes or violence. They'd study any alarms, how long it took for the cops to show up, and from which station. The elite denizens of Winthrop's City on a Hill merited cavalry, a richer response than Izzy Duncan or his neighbors would ever receive in Dorchester if they were victims of a crime.

All this thinking about robbers reminded me of Jimmy and his dog Boo.

The one fact that disturbed me the most about this break-in was that it had been done during the day. A bold act that didn't match the Lizzie Borden entry. Loot a house when someone wasn't home during the day, sure, but use the back door. Another thing that bothered me was that the Armstrongs had kept the valuable ring in a drawer.

No safe. Not hidden in a false book in the library, and no alarm system.

Izzy's aunt had been hospitalized after she experienced a mild stroke and a fall that fractured her hip. Izzy and his aunt were close. The details were spare and scattered throughout the paperwork, but they were there. His parents were drug addicts—a fact that the police wanted to make relevant—but the kid's lab results nixed that assault on his character. The saintly aunt assumed custody. She cared for him and kept him on the straight path after Cottage 9. I read Izzy as a young man who was trying to do right by the only family he had ever known.

Wrong place. Wrong time. And wrong skin color.

I noticed a convenience store. Whenever I visited a hospital, I found that I needed a breather, someplace to collect my thoughts because I disliked the damn places after seeing Bonnie laid up in a room, on my account. I decided I'd venture into the establishment.

The door to the spa was heavy, thick enough to insulate the store from gale-force winds. Silver bells tinkled overhead. Not as upscale as Filene's, Gilchrist's or Schrafft's, but it reminded me of visits to the soda fountain's counter as a kid at the big department stores. The proprietor was a big man in a tight apron. Fleshy face, gray stubble, and hair buzzed short, like he'd never forgotten the wiffle or the Fifties. This was a man who knew the differences between an egg cream, a frappé, and a cabinet. He wouldn't look at you cockeyed if you asked him to jerk a phosphate soda. His hands reminded me of a retired longshoreman, scarred and gnarled with veins. This joint was his steady income into the sunset.

"What can I do you for?"

I ran my hands over the Formica. "Haven't seen a place like this in years. It makes me nostalgic." I pointed at the syrup spigots. "Cherry limeade, please."

"Coming right up," he said. Here was a gentleman who called a pharmacy an apothecary. I scanned the overhead menu for the prices of soups and sandwiches made on the premises. Salads were verboten. The Special of the Day was the grilled cheese sandwich with a side of tomato soup and a pickle.

I thanked him when he pushed the drink in front of me and handed me a covered straw.

"Haven't seen you around before," he said.

He talked. Perhaps the absence of customers made him genial. Places such as this did well when the news said a snowstorm was imminent, and the villagers went on a rampage for milk, eggs, and toilet paper.

"Here to have a look at a place that was burgled. Armstrong residence, up the street."

"You a detective?"

"Oh God, no. Insurance adjuster."

"Figures," he said. "Wouldn't surprise me they put a claim in." He rested an elbow on the counter. "Rich folks have everything covered, you know. They live in museums, if you ask me. What kind of life is that?"

"I take it there were no silver spoons in your house."

"Silver? Kidding me, we were electroplated and proud of it."

That made me smile. The soda had the right amount of tartness and fizz.

"So what was lifted?" he asked. "I'll understand if you can't talk shop."

"Heirloom ring." I tapped my ring finger. "Big honker of sapphires and diamonds."

He whistled. "Sounds like someone's payday."

"Could be, but the cops say they have someone in custody, so there's a good chance if he talks, they can recover it…pawnshop, who he sold it to, that kind of thing shakes loose during plea deals."

"Always something for something in this world," he said, shaking his head. His eyes squinted. He stopped to pull on an earlobe. "None of my business, but didn't the cops pinch a black kid for the robbery?"

"They did. Why do you ask?"

He pointed to the door. "Two flat-foots walked in one day and asked me everything but my blood type. The odd thing is they seemed like they were going through the motions."

"Why was that?"

"They said they had a suspect, and it bothered me the way they talked."

"How did they talk?"

"Let's put it this way. They didn't use the word black or Negro. I told them I didn't think the kid did it. Look, I may not have much, but I'd bet the change and all the lint in my pockets he didn't do it."

"What did they say to that?"

"They didn't say a word, but it was obvious they didn't want to do the extra paperwork."

"They didn't take a statement?"

He shook his head. "Nope, but that didn't stop me from giving them one."

"What did you tell them?" I took out a small notebook I had on me. The guy was a model citizen and gave me his name and number before he repeated what he had told the cops.

"Kid came in often, and he'd order a cherry soda every time. He was in here the day they busted him. Said he was on his way over to The General, had an aunt in the place. Rumor is the cops nailed him at the hospital."

"They did," I said.

"Good kid. Visited his aunt like clockwork. That's love, that's devotion."

"I take it you talked to him?"

"Enough to know that we both hated hospitals. I lost the missus at The General."

"Sorry to hear that, truly, but why don't you think he stole the ring?"

"Have you seen the kid?"

"No. Only read the paperwork, but I caught the claim since this is a high-dollar case. Is there something that stands out about the kid?"

He rested both elbows on the counter now, and his hand waved me closer. I made myself complicit and leaned into the conversation. "The kid has a gimp foot," he said.

"As in a clubfoot?"

"I didn't ask him until he was in here, maybe the third time. I was afraid to ask. The kid's got enough on his plate. Know what I'm saying?"

"You didn't want to come across nosy?" I said.

"More like rude, because it's not the kind of thing you bring up in casual conversation. My brother came back from the war with half a leg and it was years before I learned the details."

I nodded. Compassion. Empathy.

He spoke in a low whisper. "The kid said he wasn't born with it, that someone got the better of him."

"My paperwork said he'd been sent to juvie hall."

His head shook as if amazed. "He mentioned it. He was sent there after he'd stolen a pair of earrings for his mother."

"Some Mother's Day gift," I said.

"Hell, it was no gift. His mother put him up to it because she was desperate for money to feed her habit. As for that reform school, or whatever you want to call it, the way he talked about the place, it was hell on earth. The guards there were sadists. Animals. They torqued his foot like it was a wrench because he tried to run away. He never went to the infirmary because they were afraid he'd say something."

"Bones never healed proper."

"Then he showed me what they had done to his fingers."

"His fingers?"

He placed his meaty hand on the counter and grabbed the middle and ring fingers.

"Bent them back until they broke." He pointed to my straw. "Kid couldn't even curl his right hand around that straw, no less use a fork."

"So he's left-handed?" I asked.

"It's adapt or starve."

I sat there and sucked up the rest of the soda until my straw slurped air. I had learned important lessons as a cop. The wealthy built walls to contain secrets and to exclude strangers. Politicians and lawyers created bureaucracy only they themselves knew and understood. Job security. One thing I learned from Lindsey was that knowing how to read and how to think was a form of freedom from tyranny. The most valuable lesson from all that reading was not what the literature said, but what it didn't.

All the paperwork from Bonnie contained truths; it excluded them, too.

Chapter Ten: One Voice, Two Messages

Back at Bonnie's place, I dialed Dot at Mercury and retrieved my messages. I kicked up my feet and watched the last light of day fade through the blinds, the buzz of the phone ringing in my ear. After I said hello and waited while she shuffled some paperwork, she chastised me for not answering the page that Mercury Answering Service had sent me. I was reminded that I paid an additional monthly charge for the device.

I informed her that the pager reminded me of something out of *Star Trek* for technology.

"Tricorder or phaser, Mr. Cleary?"

"I'm a PI, not Bones McCoy" didn't elicit a response from her. I downshifted to warm and fuzzy. "Sometimes, I want to hear a human voice. The device gives me a number. I have to pick up the phone anyway, so why don't I cut out the middleman and call you instead? If you recall, I didn't ask for the toy. You sent it."

A faux feminine sigh later, she said, "Why is it when you call, I feel like I am the character wearing a red shirt in an episode."

"Oh, don't say that, Dot. I had you pegged for Kirk's love interest."

"You don't even know what I look like, Mr. Cleary."

"The voice, that voice."

"These messages, these messages. Ready?"

I put my feet down when she gave me the number. She complained there was no name attached to the digits, but the message was "Andrea. Legion Post Four-Forty. California Street in Newton."

I wrote it down and underlined it. I had no idea why in the world Tony or his mother would have Bonnie meet the troubled Latin student at a social center for veterans. I'd thought that in addition to locking her granddaughter in a chastity belt, Tony's mother would have had her sequestered in the attic like Mrs. Rochester in Charlotte Brontë's *Jane Eyre*.

I heard the meow and looked down. It must have been telepathy because Delilah looked up at me, as if she were asking the same question.

"Next message, please."

"Says here, Bill, please call. You know the number." A pause. "You do know the number, don't you, Mr. Cleary." I said I did. She replied, "Good, because he didn't leave one," and provided the dates and times of both calls.

It seemed Tony and his mother had wanted to kick start the academic program.

The meow again. I glanced down. "I know, Dee. It looks like I'll be making Steak Diane to ease Bonnie into the meet-and-greet with Tony's niece." I looked at the date and time, and I hoped that Bonnie could make the appointment. Bonnie and Tony got on well and all, but the sudden appointment felt like compounded interest, and Tony was in a hurry to collect on the loan.

Bill picked up on the third ring.

"Tony Acosta," I said and waited a beat. "Is that name important?"

"It is to me. You got my message."

"I did. Now, answer the question."

"We're dating."

"Congratulations, Bill. The message with Dot was a personal touch. You could've called me."

"I need a favor from you, Shane."

"Who doesn't?"

"It's important."

"It always is. What can I do for you?"

"I need a background check."

"Bill, correct me if I'm wrong, but you're a cop, aren't you?"

"And you're a PI, aren't you?" he said in his signature voice that was one-third serious and two-thirds sarcastic. He relaxed the chain a little. "C'mon, it's a small favor. I'd tip my hand if someone caught on that I was dipping into the records at work. Personnel is like a clam with their files. It's one thing to ask for an address because you want to send a Christmas card, but this is different."

"Is he a cop?"

"No, but he's out and works Administration."

"And you're not. I get it," I said.

Someone who worked in Administration had access to personnel records, and he'd know if someone asked for his file. Administration provided a good cover, too. Nobody in the Boston Police Department knew Bill was gay. He was a combat-decorated veteran, like myself, and damn good on the job. Vice turned out to be a perfect cover for him. He did what they called the Fairy Brigade, which meant Sit and Wait for hustlers to try to solicit sex. He shocked me when he told me the hottest spot in town and where he collared the most johns was the Boston Public Library's bathroom.

I reached for the pad of paper and pen when Bill said he'd give me an address for the aforementioned Tony Acosta. If I had a Social, I could include a credit report.

I asked him, "What's with all the secrecy?"

"I work nights, and he knows that, but I haven't told him I work Vice." He hesitated for a second before he continued. "I haven't told him I'm a cop."

I let my silence speak for itself. I didn't have the time to hear the meet-cute. "You there?"

"I'm here, Bill. Take your pick of advice columnists—Dear Abby or Dr. Joyce Brothers—and they all will tell you a relationship predicated on secrets is doomed."

"You're one to talk. How is Bonnie?"

I had withheld crucial details on a case from Bonnie, and someone involved had attacked her. Then there was the matter of my military experience, which she was sympathetic about my not discussing, but I had incurred two strikes. The first strike was she had found my lockbox of discharge papers, citations, and medals. She said she understood that the war was a difficult subject matter. I said, "No, you couldn't understand unless you killed another human being." She said I was a jerk for saying that, and she was right. She'd used a stronger word than jerk, but that's not the point. Strike two was when Vietnam came to town in the form of a friend, Army buddy, and former CIA ghost named Hunter.

"Bonnie is fine, Bill. That was a cheap shot, and you know it. Let's try this again. What is it about this guy that has you consulting my services?"

"He's secretive about something."

"Isn't that the pot calling the kettle black?"

"I'm serious."

"So am I, Bill. It's passive-aggressive to have me run around town with a shovel to dig up dirt on the guy. If he works in Administration, how do you know he didn't look for a file on you?"

Silence. We had reached a stalemate. I clicked the pen. Open. Close. Open.

"Will you do it, or what?" he asked.

"Let's barter. There's a young man in the Berkeley Street lockup named Israel Duncan."

"I told you I didn't want to send up any flares if I snooped around files."

"Copies of any paperwork from when he was processed would be nice, or tell me what your eyes find or your ears hear. You're good at both. Put together some notes for me."

I gave the date of his arrest and the charge.

"Why do I feel there is something else you want?"

"Because there is. I want to know if there was a form for a 506."

"A strip search?" Bill said.

Chapter Eleven: Easy Night

I nixed the idea of Steak Diane because Bonnie had called to say she would be home late. When I asked her when I should expect her back, she said, 'I don't know, but I'll escape as soon as I can.' I hung up, relieved, because I didn't want to trek out to the supermarket, return, and cook, so I deferred the meal to another night. Nonetheless, she'd come home to a surprise announcement of an appointment with Tony's niece.

I resigned myself to a meal alone. Like most people, I disliked cooking for myself, so I did the bare minimum for time and quality and made do with what was inside the refrigerator. It was food, it was fuel, and I turned on the television for company while Delilah ate with gusto and ignored me.

I was three bites into a ham-and-cheese sandwich on toasted wheat, with a haphazard slather of Gulden's Spicy Brown Mustard that Jackson Pollock would've appreciated, a bag of chips, and a Vlasic pickle when the phone rang. In the spirit of spite and charm, I picked up the receiver on the third ring.

I recognized the voice and said, "Oh, it's you."

"Thank you for your enthusiasm."

Lindsey had said it with hurt feelings and a sunken voice. Like Gleason Archer, I was grateful to the professor for his generosity during and after my time at St. Wystan's. My father's suicide destroyed my mother and devastated the family finances. Since I'd been threatened with the gentleman's dismissal, the parents of a girl I was seeing had footed the tuition bill that last year, so I could graduate from the prestigious boys' school. Whatever fortune Delano Lindsey had, he shared with me in gifts of books with dollar bills secreted between the pages throughout the year and in care packages to me during Basic Training.

"I called to remind you of Silvia's birthday."

I slapped my forehead—so much for a PI's attention to details.

"You forgot, didn't you?"

I denied it as I scribbled a note to myself and mumbled something about balloons.

"Cake, Shane. We talked about this. Something from the North End, remember?"

Thirty-two years old, and I couldn't remember cake. I circled the note to myself for emphasis. "How's work?" I asked the professor.

"Atrocious."

Work has always been a safe topic among men. It was fodder at the bar, in the baseball stands, and idle chatter on the street corner waiting for the bus or subway. I joked with the man's deadlines. I offered an editorial about the local color around his office. Harrison Avenue, where he worked at the *Herald American*. Prostitutes worked one side of the street, their pimps on the other, dealing drugs from their cars. "Beasts in the jungle," I called them, but my allusion to Henry James had fallen flat because he sped past it.

He said, "The *Herald* and *Globe* are at each other's throats again."

"Age of Aquarius, age of tabloid journalism and competition. Nothing new, Professor."

"I wouldn't wrap a dead fish with either paper, but I don't like when it involves kids."

"Kids? I don't understand."

"A delivery boy came in shaken up this morning because he'd been robbed. The kid was too ashamed to admit it, but he'd been mugged and unable to pay for his papers. The thugs absconded with both his money and papers."

"That doesn't sound like management taking it to the streets, Professor. There has to be a simpler explanation," I said and waited for his response and received none, so I asked, "Was this kid from Southie, by chance?"

"He was, now that you mention it. Does it matter?"

"It does, professor. Kids from Southie would've trashed copies of the *Globe* and stolen copies of the *Herald* because they can sell it in their neighborhood."

"What's wrong with the *Globe*?"

"Southie considers it pretentious. This is a simple case of kids wanting to make fast money."

I was about to close out with the gentle reminder that I'd get Silvia's cake for the party when he said something else.

"I took some comfort in hearing that the kid's dog had gotten a few nips in before the bullies made off with the cash and papers."

"Dog?"

"A poodle."

"Was it black?"

"How'd you know?"

"Can you get that kid's name and address for me?"

My luck had turned. I had a solid lead on finding the stolen pooch. If it was Jimmy's dog, I wasn't sure how a newsie had gotten a hold of Boo, but I was confident I had found the pooch.

Not many people in Southie had standard poodles.

The color matched. The breed matched.

I hung up the phone, watched the commercial for K-Tel Records before the episode of *Barney Miller* resumed. I was unhappy that Abe Vigoda's character, Sergeant Philip K. Fish, had left the show. The actor, who looked old before his time, could convey more emotion with his eyes and his face than most Hollywood actors. If and when I wanted to rile Bonnie, I would call her Bernice, the name of Fish's wife.

Delilah secured her corner of the bed. I changed into PJs. I checked my watch. It was a beautiful night, but I felt an empty feeling when I saw Bonnie's side of the bed. I resigned myself to the darkness.

The first hour was the sleep of the dead, and when I rolled over, I giggled with glee when I looked at the clock. Nothing pleased me more as a kid than knowing I had hours to go before I had to get up for school, or work, as an adult. I breathed contentment, drifted off into the lands of bliss and relaxation until the phone rang again.

I answered with a voice that could've sharpened razors.

"They came back."

"John?"

"It ain't the tooth fairy, though I'd like to take out their teeth."

The anger seeped through the line. John's voice carried danger. I offered the fruitless and expected response, "Slow down and tell me who came back?"

"The two Irish dudes."

"You've described half of Boston. Be more specific."

"They came back, and they trashed the place. Those no good white mother—they busted up my place, Shane. It's gonna cost me some serious bread to fix the place up."

John explained how they smashed bottles of inventory behind the bar, how they bashed in boxes in storage and slashed the felt on some of his pool tables. A few pool sticks were cracked in two or splintered.

"Did anyone get a good look at them?"

"Yeah. White, angry, and Irish."

"I need more than that for a description, John."

"How's this? One of them was wearing a shiny green jacket with a shamrock near the left shoulder."

"Celtics? This isn't helping any, John. You narrowed it down to the other half of Boston."

"Okay, then I'll leave you with this fact. One of my boys was cracked upside the head with a cue ball."

"He threw the ball at him?"

"No, he went all David and Goliath on him. He placed the billiard ball inside a towel and used it as a sling. My boy is over at The General with a busted nose and one helluva concussion."

"Cops there?"

"Like they give a damn. I didn't call it in."

"Why not?"

"Because I prefer our friend's idea of justice and because the cops would probably buy them a beer for ruining my place. You need to talk to the North End."

"I did, John. I did. Someone is looking into it. You know who."

"Glad to hear it, but tell him to take fewer cigarette breaks and do more before I'm out of business. There won't be a next time."

John was serious. Deadly serious.

I told him to keep John Brown locked up and make sure the cops didn't see the shotgun.

"You don't have to worry about Mr. Brown. Harper's Ferry didn't work out so well for him, but if those crackers show up, I'm going all-out Nat Turner on their asses. You know how that turned out for white folks. Talk to our friend."

John slammed the phone down hard enough that I could feel the receiver on his end in my molars. I did know how it ended for whites under Nat Turner's *dies irae*. It was three days of rampage and revenge. Nat and his followers left sixty-some odd dead, mostly women and children hacked to death. In his anger, John had forgotten how the establishment retaliated, how vindictive they were in response to the rebellion. It would become illegal to teach a slave how to read, and Nat Turner was not only hanged; his body was dismembered at a local medical school, the skin peeled from his body and used to cover books.

I heard the door open and the sound of Bonnie's voice downstairs.

Chapter Twelve: Five Strings

I woke up early and made breakfast for Bonnie this time. I had told her about her appointment with Andrea in Newton after she collapsed into bed last night. It was bad timing on my part, but there was no way around it. I told her, and she rolled over, away from me, and I felt like the worst thing underfoot, and it wasn't gum stuck to her shoe.

She'd pulled long hours at the firm. Like most worker bees, she returned to her hive on Commonwealth Avenue with her wings frayed and her mind frazzled. Whether one wore the white or the blue collar, the result was the same, regardless of the size of the paycheck. The one difference is that as a lawyer, her work week wasn't forty hours, and the phrase or movie "Thank God It's Friday" didn't mean a thing to Bonnie because she worked weekends, too.

I had hoped to make her Steak Diane, put on a show when I flambéed the steak, but I didn't know when she'd be home, and I didn't have shallots on hand in the kitchen. When she crashed last night, it was without a word. She changed out of her clothes like a zombie and fell headfirst into the pillows, and then I told her the news.

I heard her behind me while I was conducting the orchestra for breakfast. The orange eyes of the eggs in the skillet stared up at me. The whites fluttered. The toaster popped, and slices of bread were ready for butter and the knife. The coffeemaker was done, the tank full of dark, strong brew. Bacon rested on a small rack, and Delilah's plaintive meows made it clear that she had dibs on the first salt lick.

When I turned around, plate in hand, Bonnie was sitting in the chair. Next to her napkin was a copy of *Wheelock's Latin*, the textbook that had tormented students of the classics since the Fifties. I set the plate in front of her. She picked up her fork. She still hadn't said a word.

No 'Morning.'

No 'How did you sleep?'

No nothing.

I poured our coffee. I sat down with my own plate. "How goes the Latin?"

A limp fragment of egg white hung from the tines of her fork. I chewed on toast, slow and nervous. While we might not have been chowing down breakfast like truck drivers looking to keep a schedule, the prim and proper niceties of dining between the sexes were long gone. She answered after putting the fork down and reaching for her coffee.

"I try to squeeze in what I can between meetings and reading contracts."

"They've got you working a full load while you're doing pro bono."

"Don't you know I'm Wonder Woman? Pro bono doesn't pay the overhead."

"Is the Latin ancient and forgotten history for you?"

Her finger tapped the cover of the book on the table next to her plate.

"Who can forget three genders, seven noun cases, five declensions, four verb conjugations, six tenses, three persons, four moods, two voices, two or three aspects, and two numbers?"

I said, "And a partridge in a pear tree." The look she gave me made me say, "Sorry."

She nibbled on her toast. The butter made her lips shiny and kissable.

I suppressed a smile and my lust.

"My foray into Latin was nowhere near as comprehensive as your time with Delano, and I hope she's swimming in the shallow end of the pool so I can help her." Bonnie referred to the professor by his first name, while everyone else used his surname, Lindsey or Professor.

"Andrea will tell you what book she uses, or she'll show you her textbook."

Two hands held her cup of coffee while her blue eyes studied me over the rim. "Heard from Tony?"

I was about to answer her when the pager on the counter buzzed. I walked over and picked it up. I didn't bother to look at the display. I dialed Dot, said my name, and listened to the message. I hung up the phone, rested the small of my back against the Formica countertop.

"Tony will send over a car at four to pick you up at work. The driver will take you to Newton. It's confirmed: Andrea will meet you at the American Legion Post Four-Forty."

Bonnie held the coffee cup in her hand. I gave her a few seconds for the synapses to crackle and the neurons to light up the mental switchboard.

"Four? I work until five, and that's if it's a good day."

"I know."

She set the coffee cup down. "And how do I get up and walk out without anybody saying a word?"

"They won't."

"And you know this how?"

"Because Tony said so, although technically Dot at Mercury said he said so in the message." Her eyes bulged, and I said before she had a chance to hyperventilate on me. "My guess is Tony reached out and touched someone."

Bonnie stood up. "Shane, we talked about this. It's gotta be like the separation of Church and State. This is my career at stake here, and don't tell me to relax because Tony says he took care of it. What the hell did he do?"

"My guess is he called the lawyer who had insulted you that time in the lobby."

Tony had shown up during the lunch hour and collected Bonnie in the lobby. He played the fisherman and swept her up in his net because Mr. B and I were worried that a common enemy would target her. As he was explaining to her why he was there, one of Bonnie's colleagues had the audacity to disrespect her and hand her the lunch order for the boys upstairs. Tony lifted him by his neck and pressed him against the wall. They 'had words,' which meant Tony talked, and the guy listened and tried to breathe at the same time.

Bonnie threw her napkin down. "What could Tony have possibly said to the man?"

I spread my arms. "Pharaoh, let my girl go."

"Tony would threaten the man with biblical plagues."

"I was trying to have a sense of humor."

"Good job, but it still amounts to an offer he can't refuse."

"Relax, Bonnie."

"No, Shane. I won't relax. I specifically said no direct connection between me and them."

"Them as in mob, them as in mafia?"

"You think this is a joke? Her eyes had hardened. I had overplayed my hand. She leapt to the next and reasonable concern. "Who is he sending for a driver?"

"Message said someone clean, which I take to mean not connected and not an associate."

I could tell that Bonnie had filtered my choice of words. 'Clean' meant someone without a criminal record. 'Connected' was someone with a business relationship to organized crime. 'Associate' was the more ambiguous of the three terms because it could mean someone who did some work for them but didn't take the pledge of omertà, the vow to never discuss the life. Some guys didn't take the oath because they didn't want to be on call twenty-four hours a day. If you were at the hospital, at your mother's bedside, and she was dying, you went when your boss called. No excuses.

Bonnie asked, "Is he sending a recruit?"

"I'm confident the answer is no."

A recruit was like a pledge to a fraternity. He did as he was told, without question, even if it included violence. He would act as his boss's chauffeur and drive him wherever he wanted, day or night. He was to listen and observe, but say nothing and see nothing.

"You're confident the answer is no?" Bonnie approached. "I can't have a Cadillac pick me up. I can't have any unwanted attention, Shane Cleary."

"You won't. Tony promised." She looked down as I raised my hand. "Scout's honor."

I kissed her on the cheek and wished her a good day. I told her I needed to follow up on a hunch.

The Rainbow Lounge was on Tremont, near Mass Ave. The place tried to pass itself off as something vaguely Mediterranean with its Art Deco style, its blue-and-white façade. The tin canopy over the door was as dull and glamorous as a faded nickel. The sidewalk in front had seen its share of blood and vomit. The building may have breathed gin and jazz during Prohibition, but walk into it now, and it's a mix of bad beer, cigarette ashes, and dust from peanut shells crushed underfoot.

Call it the neighborhood bar, one of the many taverns, lounges, and cafés in the South End, but the Rainbow was information central to me. Here, I could obtain news with a pulse faster than Marcus Welby, M.D. I placed a bill on the counter instead of a dime for the operator. My source was a transplant, and I had to work hard to understand him with his thick Noo Yawk accent. Grubby fingers pulled in my Lincoln. Pitted, pockmarked, and face scraped by a razor's haphazard journey, his mug looked like it'd survived a blind date with a propeller.

"Hello, Brooklyn."

"Hello, yourself. Wad youse needs?"

"Info on a gruesome twosome," I said. "One of them wears a C's jacket."

"Lots o' guys wear dem. Someone gotta cheer for the Celtics."

"These two have Southie dots." I touched the inside of my wrist, like a lady would with perfume before she went out on the town. "Before you tell me lots of guys wear dots, these two are brothers, and a jacket like that costs money."

"Jacket like that could be a knock-off. Go to Chinktown, near Tyler Avna, if interested."

"Look, Brooklyn, I'm not interested in counterfeit merch or a trip to Chinatown. I'd like to know about two brothers who've come into some green recently."

"With dots, huh?"

"With dots, yes."

I had first and last names from John, a general description from Malcolm, the dog groomer, and my own hunch that these two idiots were one and the same. I wanted to see what the operator would tell me.

His index finger tapped the counter. I fed him another Lincoln. His hand reached for it, and I covered his hand with mine. I smiled. The corner of his lip lifted up, and he exposed a set of teeth that made me wonder what woman would wrestle with him on the mattress. I marvel at how the species managed to perpetuate itself.

"Got a name for this dynamic duo or what, Brooklyn?"

"I've got a name. Costigan."

I released his hand and let him reel in his fee. I raised my left hand and imitated the cop giving permission to move forward in traffic. "Tell me more, please."

"Sean an' Seamus Costigan. Reg'lar Southie trash, if you ask me."

"I did ask you. Talk to me about their rackets?"

"Sell stolen merch through a network o' street urches."

My eyes narrowed in confusion. "'Street urchins'?"

"That's what I said, didn't I? Anyways, these kids boost stores, and they sell to the other Irish in the projects. Old Harbor and Old Colony, in particular. That's one of der rackets."

Old Colony was where Jimmy grew up and where his mother still resided. These two brothers had rocks of Gibraltar to be fencing stolen goods under Jimmy's nose in his backyard.

"The other rackets?" I asked.

"Sellin' bennies at the Illusion and other dance clubs in Kenmore. Three bucks a pill. Anything else?"

"Know where they hang out?"

"Here, dere, and everywhere in Boston, but dey don't anchor anywhere."

Brooklyn placed a pint of beer in front of me before he walked away. The Illusion was a kiddie dance floor, but the perfect venue for Art Institute and Boston University students, out and about for amphetamines for their late-night study sessions. Gossip through the Kenmore Square club scene was as good, if not more reliable than senior citizens at an all-you-can-eat buffet.

A kid would strap a bottle of pills to his leg, and the bellbottoms would hide the contraband. With little incentive to flip, underage kids were cash machines to dealers and knew it. On a good night, the little mules could sell three hundred pills each at any one of the clubs. A third of the proceeds they forked over to their supplier. The remainder they spent on fashion at Filene's or Jordan Marsh. Weekend in and weekend out until they were of age, it was a neat way for a kid to build a war chest and a wardrobe.

I took one sip of the sewer water Brooklyn called beer and left the Rainbow for Kenmore.

Kenmore Square took its name from one of the ritzy hotels there before baseball had come to town. The plot to steal the 1919 World Series and pop America's innocence was hatched at the Hotel Buckminster. As a kid, I'd stood once in front of BU's Myles Standish dorm and watched John J. Kelley gallop by to win the Marathon in '57. Once marshland and a site for dams, Kenmore Square was now home to roads, rails, and Red Sox, to scholars and students, fast food stores, record stores, and bars to suit every budget. I walked to the T station.

I was looking for the Tax Man, the King of Kenmore Square. He collected bits of spare change in a cup and dispensed kind words. His real name was Mr. Butch, and he was the start and close of the day for most commuters. He never asked for money. He offered entertainment and let people decide if they'd contribute to his upkeep by throwing money into his open guitar case. He played the Beatles, Dylan, and his own creations. He didn't harass people, and he wasn't a transient, in the traditional sense. He enjoyed a little drink now and then and toked some weed on occasion under the Charlesgate, a bridge over Commonwealth Ave.

In dreadlocks, a guitar at the ready, and a pennywhistle in his pocket, he'd greet everyone with a high-voltage smile that if it didn't warm you up or make you smile, then something inside of you was broken. He stopped playing, and his rhythm hand reached out for mine.

"Hiya, brother man. Long time, no see."

I tucked a Hamilton into his shirt pocket.

"Mighty generous of you, but you know the rules."

I did know. He gave out information in a way that didn't make him a snitch.

"I'm looking for where the Costigan brothers might hang out. Know them?"

"It is to my regret and sorrow that I know those two."

"May I ask how?"

Butch looked to his collection of bills and change. "They like to borrow without asking."

Long fingers formed a G-chord, which I recognized from my feeble attempts at guitar. He noticed that I noticed, "Country chord. Keith Richard favors it, and he only plays using five strings. Did you know that?" he said and added a strum.

"Can't say that I did."

"Tuned his blonde Telecaster to open G. Thing you need to know about playin' with five strings is you get this droning noise goin' on 'cause two chords play against each other." His hand raked the strings again. "Hear that noise? It demands rest and resolution."

"As in, brothers don't always get along?"

"You've got an ear for music, brother."

He played dissonance. Over and over.

"And how does one resolve it?" I asked.

"Move one finger or two at most, and you change the chord. Simple but not so simple."

"All because one string is missing," I said.

"All because you choose to remove the string. That high E-string is part of the standard set-up, but you've got to know what you're doin', if you want to play alternate tunin'. If you don't know all the notes or where they live, then it's war and no peace."

Mr. Butch talked analogy, and I was thinking metaphor. Not knowing the notes, how to play with or without Jimmy was dangerous music. The question was whether one finger or two would move to change the noise the Costigan brothers had created when they poached Jimmy's dog. Taking Boo was an act of war.

Butch worked through several bars, including a turnaround to signal a change in our conversation. He said, "Tell you somethin' else you might not know about Keef and his gee-tar.

Guitar players are superstitious, sentimental folks. Some of them name their instruments after what was near and dear to them. Clapton called his Strat Blackie. Willie Nelson's boy is Trigger, after the horse. BB named his Gibson Lucille. And the Keef, he named his Micawber."

His hand strummed a progression, and then his fingers picked what I knew was an arpeggio to tell me something without telling me.

Where to find the Costigan brothers.

Chapter Thirteen: Micawber

Somerville is, and always will be, Slummerville to me.

Old Glory may have first been raised on Prospect Hill there in 1776, but it has been a sardine can for students who can't afford the rents in Cambridge since forever. I took the twenty-minute ride in a cab from Kenmore because there was no public transportation to this hole. I paid the fare, and the taxi pulled away before the car's door latched.

I faced the sign for Micawber.

Its reputation preceded it like bad perfume. Even from the sidewalk, I had a bad taste in my mouth. The placard that hung from the signpost above the entrance depicted a man in knee breeches, a top hat, and a monocle. Named for a Dickens character, the bar reeked of pretension. Even worse, the sign's subtitle, Irish Bar and Pub, which was fine, but a bar and an all-night breakfast diner? I had forgotten. Wilkins Micawber had sailed to Australia to make his fortune at last for his patient, suffering wife. I shook my head. Australia—that island refuge after the British Home Office had run out of places in Ireland and Georgia for its convicts and debtors. His likeness was hanging from a gibbet here in Somerville, looking the prat, or what my Irish relatives would call a Laudy daw, a snob.

The heavy door opened up to darkness and the *l'odeur du jour* of bangers and mash. The locals went silent. I had expected as much from the 'inmates' because I wasn't a regular. The hard faces and their small, peevish eyes had to focus on the newcomer in their cave. I'd let them have their heigh-ho and raise their monocles for the gawk and judgment. Let them have a look at the prettiest thing they'd seen in a long time. I had already made one of the

Costigans near the bar. He was sitting on a stool facing the door. No small talk needed. I'd confront him head-on with both headlights.

"Sean or Seamus?"

"Who's asking?"

"Shane Cleary."

"You're a PI now, aren't you?"

The sentence flowed out of him with sarcasm and a slur. He'd been drinking.

"You could say that," I said. "I'm working on a missing-person case."

Another man joined Costigan now. It was a two-for-the-price-of-one conversation. The barkeep drifted away. The two of them, side by side, demonstrated the look I called Hungry Irish, a mix of raw depravity and hard desperation, which didn't require intelligence but a whole lot of violence.

"Missing person, huh," the second man asked.

"And who are you?" I asked him.

"Fuck you."

I was ready to play. "What, no middle initial?" I stared long and hard, ready to drop him where he stood. His friend, partner, or whatever remained next to him. I didn't see a resemblance between the two men, and the relationship between dim and dimmer wasn't clear until the bookend talked. "What is wrong with you, Seamus?"

Sean had pulled hard on his brother's arm, and he excused himself for a word with his kin. I counted a beat, thinking of Romulus and Remus and of Rome destroyed in a day. The two brothers shared a tête-à-tête that began with a low-boiling discussion and ended with Seamus spouting another profanity.

"Word of advice, Seamus," I said.

"I didn't ask you for advice."

I clapped my hands and rubbed them together. The percussive sound acted as a shock, as reveille, and the sandpapering the hands suggested planning and revelation. It was something I had picked up from Mr. B and told them, "I'll cut to the chase. The dog, I want the dog. You took something that didn't belong to you, and I want it back."

"You sayin' that it's your dog?" Sean asked.

"We both know it isn't. I get the dog back, and there's peace in your life."

"And if we don't?" Seamus asked.

He brushed his brother's arm away, stood an inch away from my face, and repeated himself, this time with teeth clenched. I was able to count the freckles that peppered the sunken bridge of a broken nose. Sean's hand reached out and pulled Seamus back.

"What if we can't give you the dog?" Sean asked.

Seamus half-turned and shoved his brother. I didn't have to work Divide and Conquer.

"What the hell is wrong with you?" Seamus said. "You stupid or what?"

"Calm down and keep your Jockey shorts on," Sean said to his brother.

I cleared my throat, and they both looked at me. "Remember me?" I said.

"Fuck you," Seamus spat out.

"You're not helping your situation," I said.

"And what situation is that?" Sean asked.

Seamus stepped forward, and Sean grabbed his brother's bicep. "Calm down."

Seamus didn't. "Say what you got to say, Mr. PI."

"Okay, I will," I told him. "You have a problem on your hands, and it's about five-eight, muscular, with distinctive eyes and the worst temper imaginable. He puts the V in violent, so I'll ask you to consider my proposition. Tell me where you last saw the dog and—"

Seamus shook an arm free. "Or what?"

I ignored his words and kept the train headed for the destination.

"No questions asked. Answer my question of when and where, and I'll take care of the rest. I don't need to know why you stole the dog. You said you don't have the dog, and all I want is answers to when and where you last saw the dog."

"And nothing else?"

"All I ask is that you two leave the dog groomer alone, though I'd suggest you leave the man something anonymous in his mailbox as restitution."

"Fuck you, fuck the dog, and to hell with your suggestion," Seamus said.

My hand snapped forward, and my fingers wrapped around the laughter in his throat. His Adam's apple didn't feel like an apple at all, more like a peach pit. I squeezed until his eyes bulged.

"You know something, Seamus. Your limited vocabulary annoys me. I'm trying hard to save your sorry ass." He sputtered while I talked. Eyes bulged. "Now, to be clear on facts. I don't care why you did what you did. My job is to find a dog. Continue to play stupid, and the next conversation won't be with me."

His body sagged when I released him.

Sean intervened. "You made your point."

"Have I?"

Seamus rubbed his throat. His eyes watered, and his face reddened.

"And another thing, don't steal from my friend in Central Square."

Sean reached down and helped his brother up.

These two delusional masterminds might've thought that Jimmy would never catch them. They were wrong. They might've thought that Jimmy would suspect the competition or, even better, think the Italians had been behind the dognapping. Wrong again.

Either way, right or wrong, Jimmy would use his pliers on them, and he wouldn't wait until they were dead because they had stolen his beloved Boo. The question was whether Jimmy or Mr. B found them first. These two geniuses had no idea that they violated an agreement between a mafia don and John in Central Square. I don't know what prompted their misadventures in stupidity, but it had turned the corner and ventured into lethal territory. They didn't look the type to remember from history class that nobody won a war fought on two fronts.

"Question for you two. Did you ask for a ransom?"

"Why would we?" Sean answered.

Seamus regained his composure; some color, too. He wiped his mouth and laughed that stupid laugh of the embarrassed. "Why would Jimmy need you?"

I stepped forward, my chest against his, our eyes meeting.

"He has his reasons. Now, tell me, what happened to the dog?"

Occam's Razor states that when presented with two or more solutions to a complex problem, the answer is often the simplest. Never underestimate stupidity, though. The Costigan brothers were what Archie Bunker called his son-in-law Michael: meatheads.

They explained.

Seamus had been out walking Boo when the dog cut loose and ran away.

Plain and simple, they had lost the dog.

Sunlight hurt my eyes when I returned outside. I raised my hand to shield my eyes from the glare. Catechism said that Lucifer was a favorite of God's, His light-bearer, the morning star. I don't know about that, but I'm certain the car I caught the briefest glimpse of a tailpipe and exhaust belonged to a Mercury Grand Marquis.

Chapter Fourteen: Bumpy Night

There was music on my walk to the elevator. Thinking of Mr. Butch, I hummed a riff and improvised on an Elmore James song. The sun was shining, and it wasn't raining in my heart.

When I'd arrived at the office, I discovered an envelope from Saul at the concierge's desk. Rather than take it upstairs, I read the message, there in the lobby. I spied Saul behind the glass at work with a client at the counter. He looked up. I smiled. Saul didn't. Perhaps Orthodox Jews lumped joy with pride and counted both as a sin. I didn't because my luck was Irish, kosher, and improving. I folded the piece of paper. Saul had given me a name and address for a fence. I now possessed a lead on that rock the Armstrongs claimed was stolen from their abode.

The life of a PI is half sit-and-wait with a phone in hand, the other half, sit-and-wait with a gun drawn. I dialed Noah, an erstwhile contact in the insurance business. I'd pitched my ask as if Nolan Ryan played for the Red Sox. Noah was a human bloodhound who guarded the company's money. Always with the scent of secrecy in his nose, he was adept at finding people and things that didn't want to be found. Tony Acosta and the Armstrong home robbery were a perfect combination of the clean and dirty that Noah loved.

Adjusters aren't too many steps shy from being private investigators themselves. There is that need for attention to detail, the relentless pursuit of the truth and, most importantly, it is a safe gig, which is exactly what I disliked most about it. Eyeballing the results of a fender bender and appraising property damages were not what stirred my cup of coffee. Instead of a real criminal, there was some guy who wanted to score some easy bucks to pay for the aluminum siding on his house. At its most mundane, someone claimed their neck hurt and visited the chiropractor. I preferred James M. Cain territory, the darker stories, such as the conniving spouse intent on collecting life insurance, or the wolf of a husband in every henhouse. Instead of a .38, the insurance man wore a pen protector, a clean shirt and tie, and lived within four walls for a cage they called an office from nine to five. All of this traveled through my mind while I dialed the man's number.

I could hear Noah chewing gum in my ear when he answered the line. He spared me the snap, crackle, and pop. "What haven't you done for me lately, Cleary?"

"Nice to hear you missed me."

"What have you got for me?"

"One easy item and one harder ticket."

The phone changed ears, and what passed for typing stopped.

"Name is Anthony Acosta." I gave Noah the last known residence. "See what his financials look like and if there's dirty laundry."

"Will do," he said. A pen clicked. "Next?"

"This next one falls into familiar territory."

I explained who the Armstrongs were, where they lived, and their recent loss. It didn't matter if his employer was the same company that had insured the ring. Insurance men, like guys on the street that worked for Mr. B, lived by a code. Their loyalty began and ended with dollar signs. The Italians added a few more virtues and vices. There was a lull over the line. I knew what Noah was thinking, but I let him lead since he was the specialist, the indemnity man.

"I'll see if they have homeowner's insurance," he said, "or if there's an individual policy since the ring is an antique. Those policies require an appraisal and leave a paper trail. Anything else?"

"Sniff around for fraud or prior history of filing claims."

"That's standard operating procedure," Noah said, sort of insulted that I had insinuated he wouldn't think to take the extra step. "I'll call you as soon as I have anything. Mercury Answering Service, right?"

"Yes, and ask for Dot," I said and hung up.

I looked around my office. It was parboiled, as in missing a certain *joie de vivre* and personality. Flush with money, I'd given some thought to hiring an interior decorator. Women allowed themselves a spa day and Tupperware parties with their girlfriends while the husbands smoked stogies, played poker or watched sports, and drank beer. My office could use some R and R, some rejuvenation and restoration.

The building's exterior dated to 1922; inhabitants such as Saul and other professionals in the gems and jewelry trade arrived in the Forties. Not a whole lot has changed since then. The hallways, for example, were papered with chevron patterns, and the one thing that made the place look less sepulchral were the cheval mirrors on the walls. The flooring underfoot were a mixed marriage of bare marble and sporadic airstrips of carpeting.

I've been to Noah's office. If his digs were functional, with its fluorescent rods suspended overhead, air conditioning in the summer and baseboard heating in the winter, then I was retro chic. I rode a solid wooden desk that wouldn't sway in a tempest, though the chair would roll on casters with the storm. The phone was as heavy as an anchor, its wire thick enough to double as a hangman's noose. My floorboards have seen history, since they'd provided the stage for carnal games between gin-soaked flappers and dime-store Lotharios. On a good day, I imagined previous tenants did everything from the Lindy to the Mashed Potato in my building. On lonely nights not so long ago, I would sometimes feel the sharp springs of a pullout, the Murphy bed in the adjoining room, where I kept some filing cabinets. The filing room was all dust, and one dead beetle from the time of Ramses II.

A grand would buy my office a face job. The floors could use a fresh carpet, something with a simple pattern that said I cared about the environment. The chairs needed replacing. I read somewhere about ergonomic designs. The Germans and the Swedes probably had something experimental, the Italians, something avant-garde. Open-floor plans are all the rage, and I could knock down the wall between the office and storage space. All of this is interior design without the cash in my pocket. I had another idea.

I checked the wristwatch. It wasn't time for her sojourn to Newton. I thought about taking Bonnie out to dinner instead of making her dinner. I considered making reservations at Hilltop Steak House but decided against it because I might see some of Mr. B's friends from his social club there. Bonnie was on the road to and back from Newton, and I doubted that she'd want to hop into another car for the ride out to Saugus. I was tempted to make a reservation at Marliave and see if I can get a table on the deck. Steve McQueen and Faye Dunaway filmed a scene there for *The Thomas Crown Affair*. I also considered Durgin-Park in Faneuil Hall, since it was close and we could enjoy the long romantic stroll to her place in Back Bay, but I settled on Locke-Ober because it was closer to home.

I dialed the number and made a dinner reservation for two. After I hung up, I called Bonnie's law firm. I spoke to one secretary before I was transferred to another disembodied voice. I repeated her name, my name, and was put on hold and subject to music before I could say more.

I leaned back in the chair as The Carpenter's "We Have Only Just Begun" romanced my ear. I liked it about as much as kids liked steamed green beans and humidity. Not bad enough for Hell, the song deserved a spot in Purgatory. After the third saccharine tune, I started to curse into the receiver to see whether anyone listened.

"Sorry to keep you waiting."

Bonnie's voice cut through the fog like a searchlight. I lurched forward in my chair.

"Um, that's okay," I said. "I think we should talk."

"That's never a good opener. I feel as if I'm in high school again."

"It's not that. I have some good news. Discuss it over dinner. Locke-Ober at seven?"

"Seven, it is," she said in a high and bright voice.

"You can tell me all about your session with Andrea."

"Will do."

I detected enthusiasm and predicted a celebratory cocktail. Bonnie's latest indulgences were either a light but sweet Aperol Spritz or the loose Holly Golightly. There's a world of difference between sweet and slutty, but at least it wasn't one of those girly crème de something drinks.

The Locke-Ober lived in a hideaway alley in Downtown Crossing. The place dated its birth to 1875. For all the infamous prudery and puritanical nonsense that made the blue bloods the laughingstock of everyone outside their tax bracket, nobody batted an eye at the nude lady over the door in the main dining room. Topless and with her wineglass lifted up like Lady Liberty's torch, the painter bothered to add a fig leaf.

Locke-Ober was tradition with a capital T, and I thought Bonnie would appreciate the place since it started admitting women in 1971. The menu was the menu, and the chef and the owner weren't going to change it. Tradition insisted that men wear a jacket, tradition demanded Paul Revere's silver for VIPs, and there was a full-length oyster bar on the first floor, a large dining room on the second, and much smaller rooms on the third floor. It was worth the walk upstairs for the private booth I had booked, the same one where JFK met with his brother Bobby and father Joseph to plan their strategy for his 1960 Presidential Campaign over a bowl of his favorite Locke-Ober Lobster Stew.

I checked my watch, and it said 8 pm.

I wanted a cocktail, a martini, stirred and not shaken, unlike Bond's order. Halfway through my drink, the waiter showed up with a small and sad plate of nuts and olives that squirrels in The Common would have shanked a tourist for, but I was grateful. It was like sympathy sex. You didn't ask why; you accepted it with dignity.

I'd been stood up.

And I lived with her, so this was awkward.

The plate swiped clean, I started to hate the burgundy leather chair, the rich red drapes, and the scarlet wallpaper because it made me feel like a bull in the ring with the toreador. I checked the time again. I felt the stares of the wait staff. Screw this.

I raised my hand.

I ordered myself a filet mignon.

Chapter Fifteen: Lucky Day

Annoyed, I stomped home to Union Park instead of her place. I slammed the door behind me, threw myself into bed to sleep off three martinis and the sumptuous meal, and woke up in a pair of shorts and a nightshirt. I answered the knocking on my door expecting Bonnie and an apology.

Long session with Andrea, the student of Latin, or not, she could have called the restaurant. Like the telegram to a mother whose son is at war, I knew the message wouldn't be good, but I'd at least have some news. The tempo of the knocks started soft as Morse code and ended like Buddy Rich on drums.

I opened the door to cop faces, rough hands, and rougher language. They yanked me out of my own doorframe, spun me around, and introduced my face to the woodwork in the hallway. A foot kicked my legs apart, and someone frisked me with hard slaps. I listened to the hot breath in my ear.

"Nice digs, Cleary. Own or rent?"

"Rent."

I was spun around in time to hear his partner emerge from the penny tour of my apartment. He whistled through his teeth, as if to say that he was impressed with my bedroom. Two more uniforms ventured inside. I could hear them make noise, like toss stuff around, hoping to get a rise from me. There was no reason to protest because I knew the chapters of their playbook. If I said one word, one squeak of protest, they'd floss my teeth for me.

I stood there with my hands behind my head. One of the boys in blue came over and asked, "What's with signs of a cat, but no cat?"

"On vacation. I'll make sure she sends you a postcard."

"Hope she has all her shots."

"Do you?"

I couldn't resist and paid the price with a punch to the gut. I relied on my time in the boxing ring and breathed through it and prayed that my dinner and the forgotten dessert of New York cheesecake would stay down. I wouldn't give them the satisfaction and double over or wheeze. Two of them stood there hoping I'd say or do something so they could tune me up. Vomit, and they'd charge me for littering and, considering my lack of clothes, add on a charge of public indecency.

"Mind telling me what this is about?"

"In due time…in due time, Cleary."

The flat feet from inside the apartment emerged, shot me a look as if I were day-old fish left out in the sun. One of them said, "Nothing. He's got a .38, and the paperwork to go with it in his wallet, along with a valid PI license. Place is clean for a has-been cop."

His partner said, "Who knew a rat could live so nice and neat?"

I was happy they didn't find Saul's note or know what to make of the name and number. Saul was smart enough not to write 'Fence' or 'Stolen Goods Accepted Here.' Find those words, a name, and a number, and they'd haul me in on suspicion of receiving stolen merchandise, and I'd spend my day as the time card for the pervs and other tough guys in the tank.

I kept my hands visible. Behind them, across the hall, an old lady opened the door. I could see her small gray head in big curlers below the bridge of links from the wood to the lock.

Her lips curled as if she tasted something sour. Like people who say they don't like cops, blacks, or queers until they meet one, she said I was the exception once she got to know me. She used to have a cat. We had discussed the price increase for tuna. Everywhere, there was sticker shock with each can, regardless of whether it was StarKist or Bumble Bee. She advised me to shop for pilchard, a sardine substitute for Charlie the Tuna.

She shut her door, and she threw the deadbolt.

"How 'bout it, Cleary. Since when have you become a slumlord?"

"Since a friend of mine named Nikos migrated south to the Sunshine State." I pointed inside the door. "Florida number is there on the stand, next to the phone, if you need to verify it."

The head cop hooked his fingers on his belt. I read the name above his breast pocket. I didn't know the name Morris, but he polished that nameplate high and bright. His companions were standard-issue patrolmen. Tall, clean, and idealistic-looking, as if they watched every episode of *Adam-12* and *SWAT*. One of them handed me a pair of slacks and a dress shirt while his partner threw a pair of shoes in front of my feet. I didn't dare ask for socks.

"We'll need you to account for your whereabouts," Officer Morris said.

"When and where is fine by me, but I'd like to know why."

"One of the Costigan brothers has gone missing."

"Missing?" I said. "Correct me if I'm wrong, but an investigation doesn't start until the person is MIA for a certain amount of time."

"Didn't know you were a clock-watcher." Morris half-turned to speak to his stooges. "We have a regular Jim Rockford here, boys." He faced me. "Yeah, a certain amount of time has to pass to prompt an inquiry, unless."

"Unless what?" I asked.

"You're a smart guy and an ex-cop. You tell me."

"Unless there's suspicion of a crime."

"Bingo," Morris said. "Why don't you come with us, and we'll chat all about it?"

"I prefer not to. Am I under arrest?"

"No, you're not, but 'come with us' wasn't a request. We can do this the easy way or the hard way. It's up to you, Cleary."

"I guess I'm coming with you."

"Smart choice."

It didn't matter what I said about my rights because the two officers grabbed me. One mumbled about having my house keys, while the other pinched my bicep so hard my arm went numb. They jostled me down the stairs. They were the delivery boys from the other A&P, the kind who bruised the merchandise and blamed the customer.

A hand tried to screw my head into my shoulders to get me inside the backseat of the squad car. Morris got behind the wheel while the other two sat on either side of me for the sandwich treatment. I was familiar with the routine. The station house on Berkeley Street was a short ride, but we would take the long and scenic route. The doors closed, and I took elbows to the ribs.

"Sorry about that," Officer Right said.

"No problem, Officer."

"Oh, pardon me," Officer Left said. "You okay?"

"Nothing like a wrinkled shirt."

The sandwich routine was something out of a vaudeville skit in Scollay Square during its heyday. It worked like this: the cop in front asked questions while the suspect answered from the backseat. If the collar didn't answer to the driver's satisfaction, then his fellow officers expedited the interrogation with an elbow here and there. A cop would yawn, and a fist flew. The car would hit a pothole or swerve to avoid an imaginary dog and the suspect would suffer more bruises and a case of motion sickness. The routine was worse if there were handcuffs on the suspect. I was fortunate that I was not cuffed, but I think that was because they had hopes I would retaliate and give them the ammo to detain me. I didn't, and I wouldn't.

Morris jammed on the brakes, and I slammed headfirst into the divider in front of me. Whoever maintained the fleet in the carpool had used Turtle Wax on the leather interior.

"So, tell us why you visited Costigan at that bar in Somerville."

I didn't answer promptly and paid the penalty. I tell my clients that cops are not your friends. It's best not to answer any of their questions. You forfeited the right not to incriminate yourself the moment you gave them your name. Forget the Fifth Amendment, I instructed, and reminded them that men in powdered wigs from yesteryear had never walked asphalt and concrete streets and sidewalks. They did say all men were created equal, but blacks and women were property then and not human beings. Words on parchment were ideals, but the streets were real.

Morris' porcine eyes blinked in the rearview mirror. Like little black beads that a taxidermist would use. "Eyewitness say you had an altercation with Seamus Costigan. Problem for you is that Seamus disappeared after you left."

There was the hook. Morris expected me to account for my whereabouts. Cops needed a timeline, and they'll edit it every which way to fit their theory about your guilt. Being a cop was about moving caseload, so the less work they had to do, the better for them and worse for you. There is no presumption of innocence behind the badge. The cat in the tree was guilty of chasing a squirrel. I kept my mouth shut. Morris cut the wheel hard as if he had forgotten a side street at the last second. I tasted olives from all three martinis.

"I want to save you time because the boys at HQ are going to have a field day when they see you. They'll line up to give you a welcome party. You know what that is?"

I did. The Army had a version of it during Basic Training. The guy who didn't pull his weight was held down and beaten with socks loaded with loose change. My class had a guy who had failed rifle inspection. We all had suffered and lost privileges because of him. He was held down and the recipient of the Spic and Span treatment, which meant he'd been scrubbed clean with soap and stainless steel brushes.

Morris clicked his tongue. "The name of Shane Cleary is persona non grata. Why is that?" Morris peered over the divider for emphasis when he asked the rhetorical question. He was right. I was as unwanted as a newborn child after the couple swore to the parish priest that they used the rhythm method. Morris invited me to spare myself and to fess up now, or become a statistic inside Holding. I could, for example, walk myself into walls and sustain a head injury, and nobody would say a word. I could fall down a flight of stairs, and nothing. In the pen, someone with a sharpened bedspring could stab me and leave me for dead.

"We know all about you, Cleary," Morris said into the rearview mirror. He used the voice heard while watching a documentary. "Yessiree, Shane Cleary is Boston's own Serpico."

The comparison was inaccurate. Years ago, I had my feet on the ground in the D-Street Housing Project in Jimmy's territory in South Boston. I was gathering intel on a victim, a black kid who had been shot on a rooftop. Everybody in Southie took to the streets after a judge ordered integration. Boston was the last holdout on racial equality. Gangs in Roxbury and Southie roved and ranged the streets at all hours. Cars were overturned, people were attacked at stop lights, and rocks were thrown at children as they boarded school buses.

Cops dished out hospitality. One thing led to another, and a cop killed a kid inside one of the projects. He swore the kid was dealing on the basketball courts. He tailed the kid and said the kid must've sensed he was being followed, turned on him, and reached for a piece. The kid was shot twice, and the cop claimed self-defense. The problem was there was no gun and no drugs, and suddenly, there was a gun and drugs.

The BPD did some housecleaning, and names were picked. It was all symbolic because those who were chosen were either slated for retirement or they were known problems. I hadn't ratted anyone out, but my testimony neither confirmed nor denied the narrative that both lawyers pitched at the jury. That I had not backed the shooter, and his story on the witness stand was seen as a betrayal of the Blue Wall.

Morris talked and played the part like he was Popeye Doyle. Eyes glanced up.

"You tell us what happened now, or the boys at the station have a conversation with you in one of the quiet rooms. You remember the room, don't you? Nothing like a private table, a good solid chair, some lighting overhead, and when you're not forthcoming, there is reading material. You remember how that works, don't cha?"

"Phone book, courtesy of Ma Bell."

The cop on my right anchored his nightstick into my groin. Cop shows don't tell you that a cop has to take the stick off his belt in order to get into the patrol car.

We drove around for forty-five minutes. They grew tired of me, tired of drawing a zero. Morris radioed in that he was coming in with me. After he docked the speaker, he said to me, "Have it your way, Cleary."

The House came into view. The BPD at 154 Berkeley Street was home to the oldest police department in the country. The place did a little of everything, from processing hookers to helping the stranded during the St. Valentine's Day Blizzard of 1940, to covering the 500 dead from the Coconut Grove Fire two years later, to responding to the Brink's Robbery in Mr. B's North End. In my time on the beat, they implemented an emergency call system called 911. Some things hadn't changed, though. The basement was where interrogations were conducted. Basements were where fallout shelters were, and where the city and hospitals kept their morgues.

I was pulled out of the car and shocked to see her.

"Is he under arrest?" Bonnie asked the two handling me.

"None of your business, lady. Police matter. Mind your own business."

"No, I won't. I'm his attorney." Bonnie held up identification.

"You coulda put a stamp on your law degree and mailed away for it, sweetheart."

"Say that in front of a judge and see what happens to you. The charge?"

Morris knew his turn at the Irish jig was over. "No charge."

"Excellent," she said. "Release him then."

The two cops coughed me forward. "Imagine that, a broad for a lawyer," one of them said under his breath, as they breezed past us and ascended the steps into the Barn.

Chapter Sixteen: Cyanide

A long minute passed before she had turned the engine over and flipped the heat on for my benefit. The seatbelt across my chest made me look like a crossing guard at the local schoolyard. Bonnie drove a bright yellow VW Beetle. I never understood German engineering, why the folks at Volkswagen put a lawnmower for an engine where the trunk was and the trunk where I expected an engine. It was a cute compact car, down to the headlights with eyelids. I never mentioned to her that Volkswagen, in German, meant the 'people's car.'

Bonnie pulled away from the curb and joined the flotilla of the many in a mad rush to go nowhere fast. While we sat in traffic, she said, "You're welcome."

"Thank you."

"Want to tell me what that was all about?"

I borrowed the strategy of kids everywhere: I asked a question before I answered one. "Want to tell me how you found me?"

"When I saw you weren't home, I called your apartment. When you didn't answer, I drove over since I didn't have the number for your landlady. She told me what she saw and heard when I showed up. Why didn't you come home?"

"You stood me up. I made reservations, seven o'clock, at Locke-Ober."

"You knew where I was."

"You could've called the restaurant and left a message."

We moved in traffic. She said, "It wasn't that easy to do at Carmen's place."

"You're on a first-name basis with Tony's mother?"

We stopped at a light. An invasion of pedestrians moved around the car like water around a stone. While we waited for the light to turn green, I said I wanted some strong coffee and two aspirins. The coffee was to shake off the hangover, the aspirin, for the aches from the car ride to the station. The light changed.

"I wish that every time there's an issue, you didn't run off to your apartment."

"I don't run, and it's not every time. You're exaggerating."

"Sprint is more like it, Shane, and do yourself a favor." She looked at me. "Don't tell me how I feel."

"It's simple. I didn't like that you stood me up."

"I was in a meeting, and it ran late, and then I was late, out to Newton."

"You can't say you're sorry, can you?"

"Like you should talk."

Bonnie switched lanes, cutting someone off, which inspired the offended party to lean on his horn for several seconds. The sonic blast acted like a fog horn in the harbor. Nothing moved except the waves and clouds.

I unclipped the seatbelt, turned sideways in the seat, my back to the window. I asked her to take the long way, as I wasn't in a hurry to get home. She agreed and said the office didn't expect her back right away. Prior to the confrontation on the steps to the station, she'd visited Israel Duncan at the station. The kid insisted on his innocence, and he refused a deal, which we both knew meant that the DA's office would visit Israel Duncan like Yahweh in the Old Testament. Bonnie would force the District Attorney to earn his paycheck and jeopardize the stats on his Win-Loss card guaranteed retaliation.

"Is your firm pushing you to plead him out?"

"You know they are," she said. "You called it from the beginning. Pro bono."

"I don't want to gloat," I said, "but you knew going in that this case was more pro forma and less about pro bono, meaning the firm expected this matter would be zipped up, locked away—no pun intended. The firm wants you back to billable hours after they get their gold star for community service. Is that what is annoying you here, or is it the merits of the case, or something else?"

"It's interoffice politics, and not the case," she said.

I played along, acted as both provocateur and supportive boyfriend. "What did they do?"

"They had one of the partners remind me I should remember how fortunate I am."

"In a word, to intimidate you, to get you to toe the line, bury the case, and move on."

We sat there, in the car, in more traffic, in a bubble that was the moment, a lull, pregnant with tension and exhaustion. Once we moved, I tried another strategy, something conciliatory. "What do you need from me, Bonnie?"

"You're the one who understands this reference."

"What reference?"

"*Ālea iacta est*. I'm looking at the river."

"Cross the Rubicon, or don't," I said.

"I'm not Caesar, but it's the same for me. No turning back, but I need help before I do."

"I need to know if you think this kid did it."

"I don't think he did it."

Bonnie parked the car. Conscientious with everything she did, Bonnie pulled the emergency brake. The sound always made me think of the farmer wringing a chicken's neck. She didn't move, and I didn't move. We sat there, in our seats.

She said, "My gut tells me this kid was set up."

"Or nobody cared since he's another black kid." I let that hang in the air before I addressed what she had put out there with the reference to Caesar. If she went against the firm's orders, she had better win the case or look for work elsewhere. I told her, "I have markers to call in. The less you know, the better."

"I'm a lawyer. Remember, I have a license I'd like to keep."

I attempted humor. "A lawyer and Latin tutor to the mob."

She ignored that and asked, "What's your read of the Duncan case?"

"What you need is reasonable doubt," I said and paused. "How about this?

100

The kid breaks into this house, steals one thing, and he legs it fast enough not only to stop for a soda, yet makes it to the hospital to visit his aunt, on time. He's there like clockwork, and there are witnesses."

Her eyes looked out at the hood of the Beetle. "What you're saying is attack the timeline?"

"Let the DA establish it first, and then dismantle it. You work in the facts such as the kid has a limp, and a damaged hand."

"Or provide an alternate theory of the crime, that the Armstrongs faked the theft."

"Harder to prove, but I'm looking into the insurance," I said.

"The firm did that."

"I'm doing it better."

She grinned. "Okay, it's back to blame the black kid."

"It's tried and true, and it works all over this great land of ours."

Her head tilted, and she looked at me. "Wait, hold on, what soda?"

I explained to Bonnie my visit to the soda fountain, how the kid had limped in and talked to the owner. I mentioned the busted hand, but nobody asked him how he'd acquired both. Not one cop, in all the paperwork, mentioned the leg or hand. "The omission was intentional."

"Why?"

"It opens a can of worms for the Commonwealth." I explained Cottage 9 in Shirley, which anybody reading the case file would see the name of the place as a mere footnote because the politicians had done an excellent job erasing it from public memory.

I told her I didn't want to go deep into details now. I mentioned that I had Noah working an angle on insurance fraud for me. Last but not least, I explained that I had the name of a fence.

"The ring showed up?" she asked.

"That's news at eleven. I don't know."

"Okay," she said. "And back to the beginning of our conversation. Tell me what that was all about back there with the cops?"

"Not now. You owe me dinner, by the way."

"Aren't you going to ask me how it went in Newton?"

"Afraid to ask," I said.

"Why?"

"It's between you and Tony's mother, and you and the student."

"I stood you up at Locke-Ober because Tony's mother invited me to dinner."

"And you couldn't say no?"

"I was too scared to say no."

"Explains why you didn't call," I said. "Did you know that she irons her son's money?"

"Freud would have had a field day in that house. It's like the Addams Family came from Italy," Bonnie said, not with a smile, but she offered one bright note. "The kid is all right, but *nonna* is one tough nut."

"Meet Tony's sister?" Bonnie nodded, so I asked her. "What is she like?"

"Attractive but bitter. I hate to say it like that, but the woman has an edge to her."

I took that in, mulled on it. "Divorced. Catholic. The family, she was born into it. All three could explain her disposition, except you forgot one thing, Bonnie."

"She's her mother's daughter?"

"That much is obvious, and I suspect that Tony will tell you as much." I thought back to what Tony had said to me when I first asked him about his sisters; he had used the word 'agita.' I said, "Think of Tony's sister as an almond."

"Why an almond?"

"Almonds give us cyanide, which smells sweet. The problem is by the time you smell it, you're halfway dead and don't know it."

She put out her hand for me to hold while she drove the car. I took in the sights of her neighborhood. Commonwealth Ave. was nice and chic, the streets as wide as Parisian boulevards.

My South End, my Union Park, by comparison, was an eyesore, a postcard of urban blight, infested with crime that came with cheap rents. There was a bar and a fight, a bookie on every corner, but it was home to me as a single and unattached man. Home was where you could stand in the middle of the street in your robe and nobody said a word about it, but still said hi when they walked by with their dog.

The dog.

Chapter Seventeen: Fence

The sign yelled PAWN. BUY. SELL, with foot-high black letters on a bruised placard above a large window crammed with tchotchkes, with Yankee silver and furniture, sports memorabilia, autographs from movie stars alive or dead at the box office. The grime on the window suggested it hadn't been cleaned in a decade. The entrance door faced South Street in the Leather District. I walked in and found all kinds of merchandise spread out like an obstacle course. Awful lighting was throughout the place, and behind the counter, fluorescent rods flickered with the heartbeat of a moth.

The man behind the steel grate made me anxious because anybody who would wear sunglasses indoors made me nervous. This vampire was either watching me or sleeping behind his shades. The dismal lighting reflected off the gaudy diamond on his right hand. I whistled to get his attention since no bell signaled my entrance.

I said the name Saul had written on his note. No response.

I described the Armstrong ring. A hand reached down and surfaced with a Colt Python, which he placed on the counter. Six-shooter, a .357, shiny and not new, and likely used. Very used.

"Here to buy it?" he asked.

"Is it here?"

"It might be. Who's interested?" he asked.

"I'd like some information."

"Then call Directory Assistance. Read the sign outside?"

"I did. Pawn. Buy. Sell."

"Thank a teacher that you can read. Now, if you aren't doing one of those three, you have no business here. The only information I give is in dollars and cents."

In the corner, a cigar Indian, the last of his people, looked laconic, because he'd been reduced to shedding tears on television commercials about pollution and the environment. I walked the length of the grating while my host hadn't budged.

I asked him, "Like working inside a cage?"

The light behind him shone like a sick halo around his head.

He shrugged and flashed white teeth at me before he spoke.

"Suppose you've got some jive about how a black man such as myself don't see the irony of working behind bars."

"Not what I was thinking at all," I said.

"Then what?"

"Cages are like fences. They serve two purposes. They keep things locked up. That would be you." He narrowed his eyes with suspicion. "And they also keep things out. That would be me."

He put his hand on top of the revolver.

"Let me remind Mr. White Wonder that I have six friends at the ready if he so much as tries to enter my world. Fool's errand, if you asked me."

"I wouldn't think of it. I'm not the one you need to worry about."

The .357 on the counter was pointed at me. "Who then?"

I turned sideways and looked at the front door. "Shoot me, and you're nothing more than another brother on the run from the police. Know how much of the benefit of the doubt they'll give you regarding your Second Amendment rights? None."

"You a cop?"

"Was. You might learn something from your friend the Indian over there."

"And what is it that you think the Red Man can teach me?" he asked.

'What General 'Fightin' Phil' Sheridan said about Indians."

"Let me guess. 'Only good Indian is a dead Indian.'"

"Substitute Indian with Negro, or black, and history repeats itself."

"What's your interest in the ring?"

"I'm not interested in the ring," I said. "Information only."

He removed the sunglasses. Eyes like Smokey Robinson matched the Motown voice. I was more impressed when he set aside the magnum. He leaned down, and I worried that he'd come up with a shotgun. He didn't. When he came to his full height again, he held a ledger book, made of black leather, its edges white and speckled with red and green. He parted the tome and ran down the ruled lines with that diamond finger. He tapped the line and turned the mammoth book around for me to read it. I read a woman's name, a Spanish last name.

"Who is Estrella Esperanza?"

The pawnbroker and I conversed like two civilized people. He did most of the talking, and I did all of the listening. In five minutes, I had a few days' worth of work done.

Señorita Esperanza was, according to the fence, a maid, or so he had deduced from her uniform under a man's London Fog coat. She'd given him an address in East Boston, which we both agreed was about as honest as Nixon's hand on the Bible. A young thing, he said, and attractive, too. Scared, he added, but not nervous. I read the date. She dropped into his shop the day after the ring had been stolen. Flew to the counter, he said, and made very little eye contact. My pointer finger tapped the single letter in the column.

"L is for loan," he said, shook his head, and closed the big book. "She used the ring as collateral. Ten grand."

"Fraction of the ring's value," I said.

"I issued her a ticket, told her it was good for sixty days, but it was damn risky for her."

"Risky, how?"

"If somebody bought the ring before the two months were out, she'd lose her great-grandmother's ring." His smile was brighter than the light behind him. "If you believe that ring belonged to her great-grandma, then that Indian over there believed the white man gave him blankets and whiskey out of the kindness of his heart."

Chapter Eighteen: Cough

Bill had the night off, so I suggested we meet at the Crossroads, an Irish pub in Back Bay. The food was fried and fatty, the service, honest and prompt. My friend Dick, the famous but neglected writer of ennui in the suburbs, held court from inside a private booth there. He might say hello, or he might ignore me, depending on how his muse was treating him. He and Inspiration were at odds with each other, polite and tense as a couple in front of the judge in Divorce court.

Bill was late.

I didn't mind. I'd have to buy him off with a beer and the excuse for not having the goods on his paramour, Tony Acosta. While I waited, two regulars near me hummed high hopes that Don Zimmer could and would turn the Sox around after Darrell Johnson got the boot. There was the question as to who would pitch. El Tiant's back was bad again, and the Sox had hired every chiropractor from here to Florida without much luck.

I flagged the waitress to set up Dick's next round. The man still hadn't seen me. Like most writers, he was self-absorbed, deep in his own thoughts. He held the pen in his hand; the notebook was open. Oblivious, Dick said nothing when she set down the small glass of water, the highball filled to the top with Jim Beam next to it. Dick's ritual was to drink his whiskey after he had stirred it with a digit. The smaller glass was his finger bowl. A Pall Mall was stuck to his lower lip, unlit and useless.

Dick had the gift. He could stomach the long, hard look at the sewer of Life and still find something beautiful in it. Tonight, I was witness to writer's block because he was staring at the blank page, like a priest who had lost his faith in the words of Christ. I turned away to respect his process.

A breeze accompanied the opened door. Bill waved at me like a long-lost brother. Nobody noticed nor cared, which is why I enjoyed Crossroads. He sat next to me and tried to get the bartender's attention. Tried.

Service from Pádraig began after he anointed your spot on the counter with a napkin. He'd tell you the lunch special, and then, and only then, were you permitted to place your order. If he was talkative, he might tell you that he had been named after the poet Pádraig Colum. I raised a hand. Pádraig saw it. I pointed to the faucet and tap labeled Guinness.

His usual spry self, Bill sat tall on the stool. Always one to experiment with new hairstyles and fashion, he demonstrated range, whether it was the Woodward look he called 'journo,' or the slicked back Tony Manero for the nightclubs. Tonight, he riffed on Bowie's Thin White Duke, as if he had hung out with Isherwood in a cabaret in Weimar Berlin, enjoying the boys and the cocaine between sets. Bill was blonde and swank in black trousers, white shirt, and vest.

He propped a large envelope against my Guinness. I undid the red thread looped around the two closures. Inside were copies of Israel Duncan's folder. All of it.

I leafed through the pages while Bill started the pint of Guinness that Pádraig had left him on the counter. I had class transcripts, behavioral reports from Shirley, and what those sadists at Cottage 9 called an 'Incident Report.' Duncan had tried to escape, but he 'fell and twisted his foot.' They apprehended him and then reenacted a version of Kunte Kinte's punishment in *Roots*. My mind continued to make associations. Bill and I served in Vietnam, and the injury reminded me of the football player Rocky Bleier, who had lost half of his foot to a grenade.

"The boys in Shirley were enthusiastic," I said.

"Read the 506 after they arrested him at The General?"

"Looking at it now," I said and perused it.

"Why would they do a Body Search?" Bill said.

"Because they couldn't find the stolen wedding ring. I'm more interested in what the 506 has to say about the color of Duncan's tongue."

"Don't you think you're looking at the wrong end of the telescope?"

I turned the top page so he could see it, and I placed my index finger next to the box. "What does that say?"

Bill's pint stopped midway to his lips. "Cherry red."

"Not ordinary red, but cherry red, Bill."

"Okay. Is that supposed to mean something?"

I slid the paperwork back into the envelope and looped the string. I set it aside and patted it with my left hand. "It does, Bill. It does."

We would've talked more, as I was about to broach the topic of the background check Bill so needed and wanted for his romantic heart, but thunderclaps of coughing interrupted us. Dick had risen from his seat in the booth, one hand on the wooden table and his other hand to his mouth, and coughed and coughed. Dick's favorite waitress happened to be behind the counter with an order. He had described her to me once. The etched lines, the hard living in her face, the utter disconnect between her visage and her voluptuous bosom, perky ass, and thoroughbred legs were, he said, proof that God had a sense of humor. 'A wicked sense of humor.' We watched Dick hack and hold his chest. His coughs thumped like an M79 grenade launcher.

The waitress nearest me said, "He's coughing up a lung from those damn cigarettes. It's what you get when you smoke two packs a day."

I said to her, "Dick will tell you he's clearing the stale air in his lungs so he can write."

"I'm sure drink doesn't help the man's health," Bill said.

I answered him. "See the two drinks in front of him?"

Bill nodded. "I see 'em. Water and a tall glass of whiskey. What about them?"

"Jim Beam," I said.

Dick coughed. His large frame rocked side to side inside the booth like a bear.

"He sounds awful," Bill said.

"He's fine. Know how I know? Watch him. If he reaches for the water, it's serious. If he chooses the whiskey instead, then he's fine."

Dick hunched over, his hand reached for the Jim Beam. He took a gulp that would've made any other man stagger. He reached for his notebook, opened it to find his pen and he started scribbling.

"Amazing that he writes at all," the waitress said and wiped away a tear from the corner of her eye. "A wreck of a human being, and he's still at it, even when nobody reads him."

"It's what writers do. They write no matter what," I said.

She was right, though. Dick was a forgotten man, both among his peers and readers.

We busied ourselves with our beers. We raised our pints and toasted to our fortunes in love. I had Bonnie. Bill had Tony. Even though Dick didn't have readers, he had a booth, a roof over his head, and a clutch of waitresses who doted on him. We finished our drinks and left Pádraig buffing the wood until you could tell which way the tree had grown before it sacrificed its life.

Chapter Nineteen: Swash

On the sidewalk to Bonnie's apartment, I gave thought to giving up my place in Union Park. I used the excuse that the apartment put me closer to the properties I managed for Niko, but I knew that excuse was as transparent as a lace curtain in the sun. I had to get over my fears, my insecurities. I thought of Dick the writer and the time he told me that all writers felt, at one time or another, that they were imposters. I understood the feeling, and I wasn't a writer.

Union Park was home to some memorable experiences, like the time I thought someone was inside my humble abode. There were few romantic encounters. Over the years, I had played host to one government assassin, cops and mobsters, and one burglar. The sight of me and my revolver, ready to breach my own residence, didn't bother my landlady either. She'd become a friend to me, a substitute mom, over the years. Her rollers out, the wave set in her hair, and at night, she smelled faintly of Ponds cold cream, and of White Linen perfume by day. She was one of those dames who worked the war effort. She said she was a badger, meaning she had worked for E.B. Badger Co. in Cambridge. She told me the company treated women horribly, discarding them when the men returned to the workforce. She crossed town to Boston's Navy Yard in Charlestown and worked there as a riveter and welder. I remember my mother telling me about the ladies who toiled in the Simplex factory making ship cable and how some of them ended up with chronic coughs from all the dirt and dust from the cotton.

My landlady, Mrs. Schneider, was a Women's Libber, all for equality, and didn't hesitate to call herself a 'broad.' She knew B was for Bruins, C for

Celtics, and the Red Sox were simply the Sox. I carried her groceries for her because my father had taught me that was what men do. I took her to the doctor. I opened up the pickle jar when her arthritis acted up. When her no-good son skimmed cream off her pension from the telephone company, I had 'a talk' with him without her knowing it. I made sure his penance included full restitution and cards to her on all the major holidays, most especially on Mother's Day, her birthday, and Valentine's Day. I'd take her out to lunch at Schrafft's on occasion, and she reciprocated with eyes sharper than a sniper at a thousand yards.

When she had notified me of Jimmy's visit the night that started the case of the missing Boo, she knew who and what he was, and not unlike Jews who won't say God's name, she wasn't afraid to call Jimmy 'Black Irish.'

I didn't take it as a slur. Black Irish were my people, but they had darker complexions and features instead of the stereotypical ginger with freckles. It's not what she meant when she said it, but I understood. Jimmy was a different kind of darkness. His hair was blonde, easy to mistake for white. The color was the source of his nickname on the street, and he hated it. Nobody dared to call him that to his face.

I looked at the door as I approached Bonnie's apartment with a sense of unease. Something was off. Everything was too quiet and creepy as an empty cottage on the Cape in the winter. Before I put my key in, I looked down at the narrow space beneath the door in search of a shadow, human or feline. Nothing. I undid the snap on the holster to my .38.

After the door to Bonnie's clicked closed behind me, I made some extra noise in the hallway to see if Delilah would come running. I thought perhaps she was asleep because she knew the sounds of my footsteps. Nope. I whistled for her called her name. Bupkis. The Yiddish word made me think of Saul, of his time inside one of the Nazi camps, which in turn circled back to Jimmy's enticement of 'personal history.'

I flicked the light on and found an unwanted guest on Bonnie's sofa. In the darkened living room was Jimmy's friend from the night I was offered the job. Mr. Construction Boots had committed another B&E to talk to me.

I asked him, "Ever hear of a telephone, or do you have difficulty remembering seven numbers?"

"Jimmy didn't hire me for my IQ."

"I can see that. You do know who lives here, don't you?"

"Yeah, I do."

"And you know what she does for a living?"

"Broad is a lawyer."

"Call that to her face, and you'll need bridgework. Why the social visit?"

"Lighten up, Cleary."

I saw the eyes, not his, but Delilah's in the darkness. When coals are hot, they glow, and heat emanates from them. The same could be said of her eyes, except it was hatred of the unwanted guest in her home, her territory. She looked like a Danish pastry on top of her favorite pillow. She stared at our guest. She wanted him gone. This lug was all shadow, no name, and his hand reached for the lamp and pulled the chain. The light revealed a regular working-class hero in blue denims, muscle t-shirt, and leather jacket. No sneakers, though. He wore the same construction boots, steel-toed, sturdy, and reliable for a stormtrooper.

"We haven't been properly introduced," I said.

"You're Shane Cleary."

"Thanks for clearing that up for me, but I know who I am."

"Nice hat in the hallway. Teardrop fedora. I've never seen you wear it. My da wore a Donegal cap to his dying day. I had him buried in that hat. He drove a cab around town. Loved that thing to death," he said.

"The cab or the cap? It's called a lexical ambiguity."

"Jimmy said you were smart, but it's dumb of you not to give Jimmy updates."

"Kind of soon, don't you think?"

"Think of Jimmy as Francis de Sales."

"The saint?"

"Saint of patience but struggles with anger. Get my drift?"

"Like a neon sign."

He rose from the chair. I kept my .38 on him. Delilah lifted her head. Our eyes tracked him as he trod across the room and into the hallway. He returned with my fedora and ran his fingers along the brim.

"I like that."

"Like what?" I asked.

"Lexical ambiguity."

"You've had your fun. It's time to beat it back to the five-and-dime, Jimmy Dean."

"You must be great on a date."

"Leave, or tell me why you're here."

He pinched the hat's dents near the crown. "I like this hat, but it's out of style."

"I'll give Jimmy a status when I'm good and ready when I have solid information."

He put my hat on his head. I didn't like it.

"Let's try this again, Mr. Cleary. See that, I called you mister. Respect. You're to come with me to give Jimmy a report. Is that clear?"

"You do realize I'm pointing a gun at you."

He parted his jacket to reveal his hardware. "We won't take up too much of your time. Oh, I forgot. Jimmy has a surprise for you." He said it with a cheap smile, and his eyes lit up. "I'll wear the fedora. Jimmy'll get a kick out of it."

We left for Morrissey Boulevard in a '74 Ford Galaxie. The friends of Eddie Coyle took him to The Garden to see a hockey game, Bruins against the Rangers, in a '68 Galaxie white sedan. They had liquored him up before they left him dead outside The Lanes, a bowling alley on the Boulevard in Dorchester.

Difference here is I was sober.

My skin crawled with déjà vu. There was something here about the car and driver I couldn't reconcile. He looked the part of a member of the Winter Hill Gang, but the car didn't seem a match. I had a good idea where we were headed since Jimmy's office was a Liquor-Mart near a rotary on Old Colony Avenue, and he lived in a modest house of horrors on East 4th Street in Boston, where it was rumored that Jimmy had bodies buried in the basement.

Morrissey Boulevard and I-93 met and braided around each other like the two snakes on the staff of Hermes, but neither throughway saved time. There was a view of Savin Hill on my left and one of the Rainbow Swash on the Boston Gas Company's gas tank. The Swash was as famous as the Citgo sign in Kenmore Square, but that wasn't why I liked it. A nun named Corita Kent had designed the rainbow splashes of yellow, red, blue, green, and purple stripes against a white background. Sister Kent of the Sisters of the Immaculate Heart of Mary protested against Vietnam; some say Ho Chi Minh's profile is hidden in the blue splash. I don't see it, but then again, I don't get Andy Warhol either. Ho used to bus tables and ate Boston cream pies on the sly at the Parker House before he made us pay the bill in Southeast Asia.

The road curved, and a moon hung wet and luminous over Dorchester Bay. A few bare streetlamps offered some light against the impending darkness. We turned onto an unpaved road. Gravel bit and sizzled against the undercarriage as the car wobbled down the path that opened up onto a field and a dilapidated shack with a light bulb on a cord inside. A profile passed the window as the vehicle came to a complete halt. My chauffeur put the car in Park and pulled the emergency brake. In this eerie landscape, weeds waved in a breeze that moved the stench of saltwater and sewage.

We got out. He was to my left as we walked to the shack.

It was like being on patrol again. I counted breaths and recited my personal mantra.

'Darkness is my friend.'

'I've known Thee in the valleys of death.'

'I fear no evil because I am the evil.'

'My rifle is my friend, and my knife comforts me.'

The door swung open. There was a shock of light and Jimmy's silhouette. The interior was stark as a shed on a lake in Michigan for ice fishing. The one stick of furniture inside—a chair—contained a man, bound, and a bloodied rag stuffed into his mouth.

Seamus Costigan.

I figured out how Jimmy had bagged Seamus. I'd seen Jimmy's Mercury Grand Marquis the day I talked to the brothers. My driver positioned himself against a wall; his hands were crossed in front of him. His foot worked the flooring, possibly where someone missed a splash of blood from Jimmy's last visitor.

Seamus sat there, silent and trussed up like a Thanksgiving turkey. The bruises and lacerations were proof that he'd been tenderized before I had arrived. I saw the pliers in Jimmy's hand.

"We were conducting a peer review. Know what that is, Cleary?" Jimmy asked.

I didn't answer, and I wished he hadn't said my name. My pulse slowed. I focused.

"You know the purpose of peer review, don't you, friend?" Jimmy asked the rhetorical question and those blue eyes drilled into me, expecting an answer, and to remind me that it could be me in the chair soon. Jimmy sidled up to me, close enough I could count the dark flecks in the iris of each eye. He spoke in a low voice. "Our friend is hard of hearing, so do us the honor, please. Explain to our guest why the eggheads at the big fancy school do peer review."

"Peer review is a form of professional courtesy in academics."

"I like that. Professional courtesy," Jimmy said. "But, you can do better than that. Courtesy to what end?"

"Verify research, for one thing."

"Anything else?"

"Verify results from the research."

"There you go. We are in simpatico now. Simpatico is such a beautiful word. Seamus here says he lost Boo, so I hope that you can verify he's telling the truth. Is he? I'd like to know because he isn't very talkative."

Jimmy held up the pliers, and between the grips was a tooth. "Molars are a bitch," he said. "I had to work hard for this one, and it's a damn shame that the patient wasn't cooperative."

Jimmy pulled out a gun. He wasn't at all dramatic about it. He eased it out from inside his jacket. I didn't note the make and model. He stuck the front end under my chin and pulled the hammer back.

"They always pull the hammer back in the movies. Why? It's superfluous as watching the bad guys rack the slide as if that made a difference. So, tell me, Mr. Cleary. Is the man telling the truth? Did he lose the dog?"

"Yes."

He didn't lower the gun. "We have verification. Now, there's honesty I can appreciate. I do, really, and truly I do, but I have another question for you, Shane Cleary."

Our eyes met. Those blue eyes had no life in them.

"Why is it you didn't tell me he lost the dog?"

I stared into his eyes. If my eyes could transfer what I'd seen and done in Vietnam, he might've reconsidered his methods, but Jimmy possessed no soul. I could've disarmed Jimmy and shot him and his colleague with his gun, but I would have a mess on my hands and a federal agent hell-bent on revenge. I had provided him with an honest answer.

"I didn't tell you because you hired me to find the dog, not who took him and why."

"But he did take my dog?"

"He did."

"And he lost it?"

"He did."

Without looking, Jim pedaled backwards, away from me. He stood to the side of Seamus and the chair. Eyes on me, he extended his arm and pulled the trigger. The bullet slammed into the side of Seamus's head, and the chair creaked, and the body tied to it fell over. There was a thump as it hit the ground. I watched the blood flow and form a small river.

Jimmy charged me and shoved the gun under my chin. I could feel heat and smell gunpowder. "Outside, now," he said.

The backdoor opened. I inhaled the sick, polluted air outside, grateful for it until I understood the sight before me. There was a lone spade, fresh earth, and two graves.

His gun down at his side, Jimmy said, "Wonder why there's two?"

"Because I saw you the day I talked to the brothers."

"You saw my car because I wanted you to see the car."

"Say what you gotta say, Jimmy, and don't jerk me around."

"Why would I jerk you around?"

"Because you're demented and because you need an answer."

"Who says I need an answer?"

"Because if you didn't, I would already be in the ground."

Jimmy smiled, but his eyes didn't. "Maybe I need you to help my colleague move the body first, and then I put you into the ground." He glanced at the soil. "It might have your name on it, or not."

"I'm not begging for my life, Jimmy, if that's what you're after."

He held up the pliers. "I can be persuasive, and I'm patient."

My chin lifted. "You must be because you have thirty-one more teeth to go before you bury the man."

He focused those blue eyes on me. "I'd like to know what you said to the cops. A little birdy told me that you were on the steps to the precinct house, but your lady friend, the damsel, rescued her knight in distress."

"You want to know what I said to the cops?"

"That's what I said, yes." His blue eyes relaxed some, and he waited for me to speak.

"Not a word about you, about our venture, or your mutt."

"Excellent. Was that so hard?"

"I have one simple question for you, Jimmy. Only one."

"Shoot," Jimmy answered and laughed at his own joke. "I'm listening."

"I find the dog, and that's it."

He blinked and held up his pliers. "Did I miss the question?"

"How is it that after I talked to the Costigans, the cops show up at my place?"

"What are you implying?"

We looked at each other, and neither of us was going to say the name of the special agent, who we both knew protected Jimmy. I could count on one hand the number of people who knew that Jimmy was a federal rat, an informant. Say his protector's name, and Jimmy would have to kill my ride home.

I took in the scene. "Water. Weeds," I said.

"Yeah, so what?"

"Know what they're both famous for?" I was within an inch of his face, and I spoke to him in a low voice. "Rats, and one more thing, Jimmy. You ever send one of your messengers to her house or have one of your goons so much as pet my cat, I will hunt you down and kill you, and I'll do it in front of everyone in Southie. Now, I'm leaving, and your boy is driving me into town."

I was a few yards away when he said, "What about the body?"

I didn't answer him, kept walking, but in my mind, I had answered him.

Bury him yourself, you fuckin' psycho.

Chapter Twenty: Enemy of My Enemy Is My Friend

I left Mr. Construction Boots's car tired, inconvenienced, and without my fedora.

The interlude with Jimmy near the water compelled me to find ethics and a spine. I needed Bonnie's VW for the drive to Somerville because it was the middle of the night, and both the T and cabs were in bed. Boston is the only city I know where Last Call for public transportation and taxis came before the barkeep rang the bell. I needed wheels to find Sean before Jimmy did. Since there was a vacant burial plot next to Seamus, it was only a matter of time before Sean occupied it.

Bonnie didn't ask questions when I asked to borrow the keys.

She had perfected the look that mothers gave their wayward charges, and she let me have it long and slow. She asked nothing, but the telepathy said she didn't think it was a good idea, especially after she'd heard me talking to Tony Two-Times on the phone. She didn't need the law degree to know that I wasn't calling at this godforsaken hour to ask for a date over a slice of cheesecake and coffee. Bonnie pretended not to have heard where I said we'd meet up.

I made two assumptions: one is that it took time for Jimmy to remove teeth with his pliers, and two, Jimmy may have cribbed from a page in the mafia playbook and had someone collect Sean for him. I suspected that Jimmy enjoyed his work too much to delegate the fun to someone in his crew. Presumption or not, I hoped that he stayed behind to bury the body.

As for the drive to Somerville, the choice was either Memorial Drive and 28 or take Mass. Ave. Neither itinerary was faster, and both required an element of luck. Mass. Ave. was a lot of stop-and-go with the lights, and I had the kind of luck that I would hit every single light. Memorial Drive was Boston's version of Formula One for the course and drivers. The speed limit was as Teutonic as the Autobahn in that the limit was whatever your car could do. There were curves and chicanes, water in the streets when it rained, and the perennial idiot for a truck driver who thought his rig could make it under any one of the overpasses.

I chose Memorial Drive and prayed for safe passage in Bonnie's Love Bug.

I returned to where I had first met the brothers in the hope that Sean was a creature of habit. I didn't see him, so I asked around. The faces were harder than usual, and there was no love for me in any of them. The brothers had besmirched my name in absentia. I knew I had to be economical for time and decisive. I quit the scene because it gave me nothing, and nothing invited insult more than the sight of a man who drove a Beetle looking for another man. It might pass in Bill's world, but I wasn't sticking around to test the theory.

I stepped outside. It was dark, and the neighborhood had nothing to brag about for the tourists. It was nighttime. Most people were asleep inside their triple-deckers. Each floor, each layer of the house, was a sandwich that housed a generation of working-class Irish, Italian, and a smattering of Canadians. Folks here worked at what manufacturing plants remained or what the construction of I-90 hadn't destroyed. Property taxes were some of the highest in the Commonwealth, so simple economics drove residents to the suburbs.

Somerville was Contract City, as in a contractor's paradise. Everyone took what they could of the city's money. Like an auto chop shop, the politicians would dice up contracts into smaller pieces so they were too small for bid contests. Another end-around was to declare a job an 'emergency.' Walk or drive, you'd see the same signs for the same contractors. Fraud was in the genes and in the drinking water.

I spotted a packie and decided I'd ask the proprietor where I could find Sean Costigan. It was worth a shot, even though I understood that in a small village, the villagers protected their own. Enemy or friend, Irish or Italian, it didn't matter. There were five zip codes in Somerville, but they all amounted to one common seven-letter word: loyalty.

I pulled the door, heard the jingle overhead. The owner gave me the once-over. The eyes were neutral, but the thought across the wires inside his head said I didn't belong. I wasn't from the Ville. I was no Villen. I made no pretension to schmooze and talk to him. New Englanders are notorious for blunt conversation.

"I'm looking for Sean Costigan. It's important."

"Everything is important," he answered, voice raspy from decades of chain-smoking Camels. An oxygen tank was in his near future, and he was the guy at the VA Hospital who went outside in his wheelchair, tank strapped to his rig, tubes snaked into each nostril, and the cig clamped between his lips. I saw the tattoo on his forearm.

"You're a Navy man," I said and pointed.

"You don't look like a squid to me."

"No," I said and added, "I was a grunt. Vietnam."

"A dogface then. It could be worse. I served in the Big One."

"I'll cut to the chase, Sailor. I'm trying to save Sean's life. If you don't know where he is, then say so, and I'll be on my way. I need to move fast, or he dies tonight."

"And you're Mighty Mouse, here to save the day."

"Day is gone, friend, and there aren't many hours left to the night. If I don't find him, he ate his last meal tonight, if he had one."

The old buzzard coughed the smoker's cough. "Ham and turkey. He ate ham and turkey." He pointed to the shiny slicer. "Sandwich, a bag of chips, and a six-pack of Schlitz. He came in about forty-five minutes ago after a night of drinking. We had our usual banter." He coughed again and wiped his mouth with a grody handkerchief. "I tell him he drinks too much, and he says I smoke too much. I tell him to fuck off, and he says fuck off."

"Happen to know where he went?"

He pointed to a triple-decker and indicated the floor and which door was best for success.

"You've done a good deed on your watch, Mister."

"Don't be too quick to thank me. Sean is on his second hangover with that six-pack. He might be a little feisty."

"Feisty is better than no pulse." I thanked him again, and headed out the door.

There was a stack of old newspapers, so I took one and rolled it up. People used it to chastise the dog, but it served two potential purposes. I could jam it into the open space before he closed the door, or I could use it as a club to show Sean the errors of his ways. As I expected, Sean answered with attitude and tried to slam the door shut when he realized it was me.

The copy of the *Somerville Times* worked like a diaphragm did for birth control; it provided the barrier I needed and blocked the door from closing shut. Sean was all protest and suds. It was better that he had had a few under his belt because it would desensitize him for what was coming later.

I told him we were going for a ride. He exhausted all the profanities he knew from parochial school. He asked why, and he thought my answer was melodramatic. I assured him that, if anything, I had downplayed the severity of the situation. He mentioned that he'd like to call his brother. I said it was late and we didn't have time.

Sean cracked wise about Bonnie's car. "Is this your idea of Stranger Danger? No amount of candy you have would entice a kid to get into this vehicle."

I asked him if he knew where the trunk was on a VW, and he said that he did. I told him that I was disappointed because I wanted it to be a surprise when I stuffed him into it if he persisted with the insults.

We drove and drove. Like a kid, he squirmed and fidgeted, touched the dial to the radio a thousand times. I said nothing for the twenty-minute drive. He whistled and hummed until he attempted conversation. "Are you putting me up in some kind of safe house?"

"Something like that," I answered.

"For how long do I have to lay low?"

"For as long as it takes."

I didn't have the heart to tell him that the safest place for him was the hospital that Tony Two-Times would put him in, and the duration of his stay equaled the time it took for him to recover from the penalty for his bothering John and violating one of Mr. B's 'friends.'

Sean didn't need to consult the Road Atlas to realize that our destination was the North End. He turned to me in a panic. "You're handing me over?"

"Safer for you this way."

"How in the hell is it safer for me?"

"Because you, my friend, don't have many choices. It's either the guy whose dog you lost, or it's the Italians."

"You're handing one of your own to the greaseballs...what are you, Judas?"

We'd arrived, but he didn't know it. I pulled to the side and jammed on the brakes.

"No, I'm not Judas. I'm Pontius Pilate. I decide whether you live or die."

He jumped when there was a knock on the window on his side of the car. Tony Two-Times.

His face was sheer panic, the kind the toughest inmate experiences when he sees the electric chair in Charlestown State Prison, where Sacco and Vanzetti met their end.

"You can't be serious?" he said.

"Don't keep the man waiting, Sean. He needs his sleep, too."

"But he'll kill me. You gotta know that."

I reached over and cranked the handle to lower the window. Tony bent over and looked at the catch and then at me. I asked Tony, "Our friend here thinks you're going to kill him. Tell him you're not going to kill him."

Tony looked at Sean and said, "I'm not going to kill you."

"And I'm supposed to believe you."

"I'm a man of my word."

"What then?" Sean had calmed down some, seemed somewhat resigned to his fate. He asked the question twice, once of Tony and then of me.

Tony answered. "What you did in Central Square wasn't very nice, and there's a price to be paid."

"What's the price?" Sean said. "If it's money, I can—"

"Save your money for the hospital bill. Let's go, get out of the car. We'll make it quick."

Tony's large hand rested on the car frame, which freaked Sean out. "I'm gonna die."

I leaned over. "Tony, explain to him why he isn't going to die."

"Simple. You interfered with business. We put you in the hospital for a few days. Think of it as a vacation."

"You're gonna hurt me."

Tony smiled. "You won't feel a thing. Later, I'm not so sure, but the upside is hospitals are where the painkillers are, so it's win-win for you."

Sean glanced over at me. I nodded. "This is better than the alternative. Take the deal."

Sean opened the door. Two guys behind Tony stepped out of the shadows. Sean stood there, meek and mild and docile as the lamb before the pagan's altar. Tony thanked me and assured me that they'd tune Sean up. Tony hinted that he had it down to a science, the number of days it'd take in the hospital for the penitent to complete his recovery.

Tony ducked down for a final word. "No worries. He'll live. Mr. B appreciates this. This goes into the book, next to your name, and that's a good thing."

I pulled away and let the night swallow me and the Beetle. Killing Sean would be bad for business and pointless. A hospital was the safest place for him. He'd receive medical care, and he'd be forced to stop drinking for a few days, enjoy three squares and a luxury bed.

An Irishman was safer with his enemy than with his own.

Chapter Twenty-One: Not Good

I felt an awful pressure on my chest that was easy to mistake for angina. Delilah had climbed on board, either to remind me that her breakfast was late or to remind me that I was her private pillow. I read somewhere that cats fixate on their human owner, and they enjoy the rhythms of their breathing and heartbeats as a way of remembering their mothers.

I opened my eyes, took in the ceiling, and ran my hand through her fur. I closed my eyes and listened to Delilah's soothing purr. It stopped for a moment, and then I experienced a head butt as the memo that it was time to rise and shine.

I shut my eyes and received a paw to the side of the face.

It couldn't have been food because Bonnie would have fed Delilah before she left for work. If Bonnie had said something to me or kissed me before she left, I had no recollection of either event.

I received another feline slap. I turned my head and hoped for a note from Bonnie and found none, though I did see the pager from Mercury Answering Service. I realized Delilah's attempts at lulling me away from Lethean fields were her way of saying I had messages from Dot at the Service. Had Delilah been a dog, she might've grasped the pager in her jaws and dropped it on me. Since she was a cat, more independent and less inclined to please, she swatted me to remind me to do it yourself.

I shooed away an annoyed cat.

The pager said I had messages.

I stretched the cord and fumbled with the phone, grateful for touchtone dialing instead of the rotary dial I used to use as a kid. My finger sprinted through the seven numbers, and I listened to the tone. I recognized her voice and said hello to Dot.

"You have three messages, Mr. Cleary."

"Three separate calls, or same person."

"Same person."

There was a lull on the line. I didn't hear her reach for something, and she didn't advise me to fetch pen and paper, so I asked, "What's with the silence?"

"I want to play."

"You want to play?"

"We've always had fun when it came to this part of our relationship."

"Relationship is a recurring word in my life these days."

"Excuse me?"

"I haven't had my morning coffee, Dot. I'll play. A clue, please."

"He is someone who would need two of everything for the boat."

"Noah?" I said and shifted in bed. I sat up and rested against the headboard.

"Correct. Look like you won this round of Password."

"Pyramid is better. I'd pick Dick Clark in a knife fight over Allen Ludden any day."

"Noah says to call him. He has some information for you. I have his number."

I recited Noah's digits from memory. I asked her whether that was the number he left in triplicate with Mercury. She said I had it right, times three. "It must be urgent if he called you three times, Mr. Cleary."

"Noah is persistent, if not insistent. The better clue next time is the father of the American dictionary."

"Noah Webster?"

"We have a winner," I said and hung up the phone.

I sat there. Delilah stared at me. Her eyes opened and closed as if she wanted to hypnotize me. I wanted more sleep. I needed it, but I couldn't afford it.

Jimmy shot a man over a dog. He killed Seamus for dognapping and losing the pooch. I'm certain that Jimmy forced Seamus to dig his own grave plus one before I arrived. When he asked me about the visit from the cops, I was confident my answer had saved me from that second grave. I would've resided there for all eternity, unidentified after Jimmy performed dental work on the both of us.

The phone rang again. I picked it up and garbled a hello.

It was Bonnie.

She used her business voice, nice and straight to the point. Bonnie wanted to know whether I had any new news on Duncan's file. People weren't people to lawyers; they were a 'file' or a 'case,' but I've been guilty of the same offense myself because I dipped into the lexicon to establish distance. I acquired the skill in the military, where we had all kinds of code for casualties. Cops do it all the time, too. Bill had given me the 'jacket' on Israel Duncan. Noah's world used all kinds of words. People were not people; they were claims and policy numbers.

After I'd hung up, I was uncertain whether the tone of her voice registered disappointment in the lack of progress on her client or it could be that she was busy at work. I sat there. Delilah lay next to me.

The phone rang again.

The voice again.

"Where the hell have you been?" he said but didn't wait for an answer. "I've left you a million messages and—"

"You've left three, Noah. Three."

"You don't sound so good."

"I'm tired, I'm cranky, and my cat is annoyed with me."

Delilah took to kneading me. She tenderized my flesh with her claws. She purred while her talons exercised a rhythm of pull and release. Noah told me to listen, and I did. He said he'd take it from the top. He did. He recited the pertinent facts about the alleged robbery. Saul was on the nose about the ring's value. Hundred-grand-insurance policy. Noah zeroed in on Israel Duncan. If the suspect helped recover the lost property, he said insurance companies talked leniency and encouraged a plea deal with the lawyers.

Noah said, "Everybody wins. The court saves time. Property is recovered. Instead of a cash reward, it's less jail time for the thief." He told me he had a theory about the Armstrong couple.

I asked, "You found something fishy?"

"I did. But let me explain something first." Noah held the phone close. I could hear him breathing. "All insurance companies drag their feet on paying out," he said. "The Armstrong couple wouldn't see a dime for at least a year. Their fins say they're hard up for cash."

"'Fins'"? I said.

"Their financials. They have money, but they're not liquid."

"They're short on cash then," I said.

"Correct." Papers rustled. "I found something intriguing. They let go of the help. A maid, specifically." He read the formal name from a piece of paper and said, "Why do Spanish names have to be so damn long? I can't pronounce any of this."

Delilah's claws dug in.

I asked him for the first name, though I suspected that I knew the answer.

"Estrella," he said. He pronounced the double L in her name the Anglo way instead of as a Y. "Lady gets the boot, and the bank records show a modest cash withdrawal."

He named the amount. "And how do the Armstrongs explain it?" I asked.

"They said it was severance and the least they could do for an employee who'd been with them for years."

Like a loud ping pong ball, the word 'severance' bounced around inside my head. I returned to Noah. "But you're not buying it."

"Nope. My investigator says the husband admitted to having an affair with her, but didn't want the missus to know about it, but we both know wives always know. There's the stink, and there's more fish."

"How much did he pay her?"

"Five large to go bye-bye."

"Hush money is cheaper than a divorce, Noah. You've seen it before, no doubt."

"Oh, but it gets better." He paused as if he expected a canned drum roll for the studio audience. "She's nowhere to be found. No paper trail anywhere. Your thoughts?"

"The rich hire illegals to avoid all the taxes. I'm thinking two things, as in she went back home, wherever that is, or she is somewhere in Boston under another name."

"I'll speak with my people at Logan and INS."

I could've told Noah about the fence, about what I had learned there, but I didn't. Delilah had settled in. I inquired on another matter. "Anything on Tony Acosta?"

"Not much to tell, Shane. The kid is clean. If he has any secret, it's that he's attending classes for his GED. You know the deal. Get your diploma and find a better job, or so goes the lie. I dug around his employment history. Tony has been everything from a dishwasher to a grease monkey. Could be he's tired of dishes and carburetors." I heard Noah tap a pen or pencil. "You'll love this, Shane."

"What?"

"His current position is in Administration within the Boston Police Department. You don't need a high school diploma for his job."

"You do if you want to move up the ladder. How did you find out about the classes?"

"I have my ways." He said it with pride. "You're not the only one who plays detective."

I congratulated him and told him I'd be in touch. Delilah was comfortable, head resting on her paws, eyes closed, and her tail curled around her body. She slept through the ambient sounds of the neighborhood. Kids outside played. Across the street, a foreign couple argued. He was yelling in one language, she in another, but they both understood each other.

I reviewed the scenes in my head. Seamus Costigan was sleeping in a ditch. He snored through the hole Jim put into his head. Brother Sean would soon enjoy a stay in Somerville Hospital, and if Tony and his friends were too thorough, he might be moved to Massachusetts Rehabilitation Hospital for physical therapy. The couple across the street were well into their second round.

Russian. The man was yelling at his wife in Russian. She returned fire in Yiddish. Somebody had thrown a plate. He launched a salvo. She responded with another dish. Breaking glass was affordable therapy for those who couldn't afford marriage counseling.

Someone thumped the door. I recognized the cadence.

Police.

I moved Delilah. I jumped into a pair of jeans. I pulled on a long-sleeved t-shirt.

They were drumming the wood until the light around the doorframe had a heartbeat. This had better be good, I told myself as I opened the door. I knew better than give them lip. Let them talk first.

It was a lead cop with a trio for backup. These were experienced cops, the seasoned dogs that the captain would send after the wolves in the wilds of Mattapan or Eastie. The frontman was the familiar Officer Morris. The three policemen behind him said nothing. If I so much as moved the wrong way, they would carry me out like furniture.

"This is about Seamus Costigan," Morris said.

I didn't answer. He was enjoying this, playing the voice of *This Is Your Life*.

"We've got it on good authority that you shot and killed him."

I turned my head to the holster on the coat rack. "You're welcome to run ballistics on it." I showed him my hands. "If you like, you can test my hands for gunpowder residue."

"Don't have to," he said with a slick smile, "because your old service piece, the one you used when you were on the force, was a match."

"You mean the one the BPD took when I left the force. Thought it was destroyed."

"Got an answer for everything, Cleary," he said.

He wasn't done, and I knew it.

"You match the description."

I responded. "Gun, a body, I presume, and there's a witness. How convenient."

"The description is what sold us. Right, boys?"

The trio didn't blink. They eyeballed me as if I was sirloin on Saturday night.

"Who else do we know wears a fedora?"

Mr. Construction Boots had made off with my hat and left me with the

131

ticket.

"Charging me?"

"Not yet. We want to have some fun with you first. Watch you squirm like a worm."

"Let me get my coat. Off to the station we go."

"No," he said. Another sick and sadistic smile. "We're taking you somewhere special."

The three cops, six arms, swallowed me up.

Chapter Twenty-Two: Spades

T he late Otis Redding sang about sitting on the dock of the bay. I was standing instead of sitting, handcuffed. There were no ships to watch in Dorchester Bay. A few white boats bobbed in the drink, along with some fat seagulls. A few crows circled and cawed overhead. The Evidence boys were busy with spades.

The perimeter was established with sticks and cordoned off with tape, the kind used for crime scenes. The wind off the water whipped against our jackets as the Forensics team pierced the earth and made wet slapping sounds, moving dirt. The diggers worked a dirt square. It was obvious that the ground had been violated twice, and the soil tilled. The only thing missing was Leonard Nimoy's voice saying, 'In Search Of Seamus Costigan.'

The handcuffs cinched tight around my wrists. There was no buffer against the mix of brine from the bay and the smog from the planes into Logan Airport. There was no sun. Only dampness and stench. The three cops around me stood impassive. That would change when the archeologists found their prize. My former alma mater, the BPD, cherished grudges, remembered every slight like an immigrant mother, a vindictive ex, and a nasty boss rolled into one. Morris claimed a Ballistics match tied me to the murder weapon, but that made no sense, so he might as well have been talking to me about the single bullet that killed Kennedy and wounded Governor Connally. A ballistics match meant a bullet inside a body matched the lands and grooves that the murder weapon produced.

Every police department kept a signature of each cop's service revolver on file, whether the cop was living, dead, or retired, because weapons do get stolen and cops go rogue. Either way, someone had dropped a dime and told them that X marked the spot, that Seamus Costigan could be found here.

Two homicide detectives emerged from the shack. Two nerds from Forensics with cameras around their necks were in tow. They looked disappointed. I've worked with technicians, and the smallest things would excite them. These two looked as forlorn as two teenagers after the condom had broken.

The lack of physical evidence was good news for me. Homicide detectives and lab rats searched for the slightest clues, such as fabric, fibers, hair, and blood. The lead detective led the parade past us, shaking his head, as if to say he and the crew had found nothing.

Nothing.

Zero was a real number.

Morris, the lead cop, turned to me. "Don't think you're in the clear."

He tagged a date and gave a window of time large enough for me to fly to Italy, scale a ducal palace, steal a Leonardo, and fly back with enough time for a breakfast of scrambled eggs and caviar with champers. "What do you have to say for yourself, Cleary?"

"I wish to speak to my lawyer. Her name is Bonnie Loring."

"Say something?" Someone's hand took hold of the cuffs and twisted them.

"I said I invoke my right to an attorney."

There was silence because someone had shouted that they thought they found something. The diggers were casket-deep into broken ground. They had piled up black soil in a nice, neat mound. Perhaps instead of the standard mafia hit of a bullet behind the ear, body dumped in a shallow grave, they expected a fresh corpse in an old oil drum or a pit lined with lime. The chain gang continued their cadence of spade scratch, lift and dump.

"Never mind," a voice said from the pit.

Morris returned to his sketch. "I keep thinking about that fedora of yours."

He had said earlier that somebody had seen me wearing the hat. If this witness had been on a boat in the bay, visibility was crap at best. Morris would have a grand jury believe that a witness had seen a man, hat on his head and gun in his hand, shoot and kill someone and then bury the victim.

Morris was riding with it, because cops are allowed to lie to suspects, thanks to Frazier v. Cupp in '69, and he had nothing to lose. The two cops on either side of me acted as pillars. I didn't know if the plan was to spatchcock me or brace me for a fist sandwich from Officer Morris.

"A fedora is old-school, doncha think?"

I answered him, "You should stake out Coolidge Corner."

"Why is that?"

"All three versions of *The Maltese Falcon* are playing there this week. Buy yourself a bucket of popcorn and count how many fedoras you see there between matinee and last show."

Morris sucker-punched me, but I had anticipated it and braced myself like Houdini would for his fans. I hadn't forgotten that Harry died from a lethal punch to the abdomen from a college kid. Ruptured appendix. I wouldn't give Morris the satisfaction of hearing me gasp or double over.

"Hey, we found something," one of the diggers shouted from the pit.

Someone behind me pulled my head back to whisper into my ear.

"After we're done with you, you'll wish that you were in that hole in the ground."

That someone in my ear yanked the cuffs up and pushed me forward. My shoulders hurt like hell. Morris led the way until he stopped and turned to me. "Last chance to say something."

"Sure," I said. "Two words, seven letters. Wanna guess?"

It was worth the pain. Morris didn't punch me this time. His partner behind me drove his knee up between my legs. He let me fall down to enjoy my private agony, which, with the handcuffs on, would make standing up fun. My face in the weeds, I coughed and tasted dirt until a good officer tipped me over with his foot and rested his heel on my chest.

One of the techs came into view. "Never mind," he said. "Nothing but a big stone."

His partner climbed out of the hole. "This is a total waste of time."

Morris said to the diggers. "Didn't someone say they found a set of footprints?"

The footprint on my chest hadn't moved; the handcuffs underneath me dug into my lower back. A technician lifted my leg, examined my foot, and dropped it.

"Not a match for type of shoe," he said.

"Are you sure?" Morris asked.

"The prints we photographed belonged to a pair of construction boots."

A flustered Morris said, "He could've changed out of them."

"Even if he did, wrong size foot."

Morris stamped his hoof and muttered a profanity. 'Lucky Mick' was the tame half of it.

The technician explained it to Morris, and I enjoyed the theatre as a groundling.

"We're looking for construction boots, steel-toed, and given the impressions in the soil, the person who walked through the scene was taller and weighed more than your suspect on the ground here. In simple terms, no match to the evidence. Therefore, no collar."

There was another voice. Bonnie? I couldn't see around the leg on my sternum.

Morris spoke. "You again?"

"First on the steps to the station and now here. We have to stop meeting like this."

"I'm curious, Miss. How did you know to come here?"

"I have ESP. Now, correct me if I heard wrong. You have no evidence, correct?"

"Correct."

"Any indication of foul play, yes or no?"

"No, but we can question him."

"Look, Officer."

"Name is Lieutenant Morris."

"Bonnie Loring, and I'm not happy to make your acquaintance. Did this man ask for his lawyer?"

"Yes."

"You know once any suspect asks for a lawyer, the wheels stop."

"You should be flattered because he asked for you by name."

"What can I say, Lieutenant? Shane Cleary knows how to make a girl happy, but you know who isn't going to be happy with you? I'll tell you: a judge."

"I did this by the book, lady."

"It's Counselor, Lieutenant, and you best remember the distinction. Threaten my client?"

"Threaten him? We talked."

She looked to me and smirked when she focused her attention on Morris again.

"He's on the ground. You're standing. Am I missing something?"

"We can question him, Counselor."

"You may, but only in my presence, and at the station house. What will it be?"

Morris gave the order. "Cut him loose."

I was rolled over like a side of beef, and the handcuffs were unlocked. I got to my feet and rubbed my wrists. The expression on Bonnie's face could've scared off the Medusa. She wouldn't look at the cops and technical team as they filed past her. She kept her purse slung over her shoulder. What little sunlight there was lit her blonde hair platinum.

"Sorry if you ruined your shoes in the weeds here," I said.

"I don't mind. I walk through bullshit every day, including yours. Are any of them looking at us?"

I looked over her shoulder. "No, why?"

I wasn't fast enough to avoid the purse to the side of the face.

"What the—"

She hit me again with the bag. Whatever women packed in those things was heavy, and it hurt like a sock filled with billiard balls from John's bar. "Why didn't you tell me?" she asked.

"Tell you what? You were at work. I didn't have time to call you."

"I don't mean that, idiot."

"What then?"

"Working for Jimmy, for starters?"

"How do you know I'm working for him?"

"Because I don't hear you denying it."

"You're a lawyer, Bonnie, and it's better to have distance, remember?"

"But Latin tutor to a mafia princess is okay?"

"How did you find out?"

My brain ran through all kinds of calculations, but the cash drawer didn't open until I arrived at one and only one answer. Stunned, I dropped my hands. "He called you?"

She walloped me with the purse. "At the firm, Shane."

"Nobody can't say that he doesn't have a pair."

"What kind of case could you possibly be working on for that monster?"

"Finding his dog named Boo, and that's the truth."

"You'll explain the rest over breakfast. Your treat."

Bonnie started to walk away when I called out to her. She turned around, and I asked her,

"He said his name?"

"Of course not, you moron."

"Then how did you know it was him?"

"Evil has a voice."

Chapter Twenty-Three: IHOP

Bonnie decided on the IHOP on Soldiers Field Road instead of the one in Kenmore Square. She said we needed lots of empty space and a quiet booth where we could talk. She was right. Kids undecided on their major, kids working off hangovers from a night at The Rat, and kids with post-coital regrets flooded the HOP in Kenmore. Breakfast in Brighton promised privacy.

Soldiers Field Road remains a pioneer stretch of road, a series of bridges across the Charles River where a slaughterhouse once dumped offal. The abattoir was gone, dead as the cattle killed there. Miles of gray cracked asphalt and a faded divider line made driving treacherous. Every now and then, some wily pedestrian attempted to cross the dangerous expanse and made the news for his fatal endeavor. On summer days, there was no shade or sanctuary. The linden trees have since died. The junipers struggle. When it rained, the sides of the road washed away into mud.

The demographic for this IHOP was different. Seniors frequented it. The food was consistent and cheap, the service courteous and efficient, and the menu predictable as the traffic of truck drivers, who hauled guns for the IRA out of Brighton.

The waitress handed us laminated sheets. Bless her for not judging. One side of my face looked like the hash on the menu. My mouth tasted like toast. My chest ached, and my wrists were raw. One look at us, and she might have thought of us as the parolee meets with his PO. I wanted endless coffee.

Bonnie hadn't said a word on the drive over. Not one. She'd stared straight through the windshield, while I debated the farmer's breakfast or waffles.

I avoided eye contact. Whether she had depositions, court dates, or meetings with the boys in the office, I don't know. Jimmy called, and she jumped. I wasn't foolish enough to exercise idle talk. If I were to compliment her on how she looked, I'd be ingratiating myself with her and playing the artful dodger. If I were to open up my defense as to why I took the gig from Jimmy, she'd disassemble my logic before I tasted my breakfast order. The waitress set down large mugs before she left, and I batted my eyelashes over the rim of my coffee cup at Bonnie. She shook her head. "You're something, you know that?"

Her hair was pulled back. Someone somewhere had written a manual that said women couldn't keep their mane long in the workplace. Femininity was wrong, masculinity was power, and the war cry was as Shakespearean as "Unsex me here." I found this rather perverse and ignorant. In the ancient world, long hair symbolized strength. Achilles of the Greeks, the Vikings, who were Bonnie's ancestors, all wore their hair long, defiant, on display, and with pride. Short hair was the sign of the defeated, of slaves, and the humiliated. As for women, numerous classical authors, Greek and Roman, wrote about how Celtic women stayed behind, armed with a dagger. If their male kin fell in battle wounded, she was duty-bound to journey out to him and slit his throat so the enemy wouldn't hold him for ransom. In addition to long hair and ferocity, Bonnie shared another trait with Celtic warriors, and that was she liked the color blue. The Celts ran into battle, long sword in hand, naked, and their bodies painted blue.

Bonnie's ensemble was a closet full of Chanel suits from a consignment shop in Watertown. She had them tailored, and she maintained them as if they belonged in the Smithsonian. Except for a simple chain around her wrist, she was blue, cold, and sexless.

Our dishes arrived.

French toast for her, waffles and bacon for me. The common denominator between us was the choice from the syrup caddy. We both had reached for it. My first mistake was to apologize. My second was to believe that the gentleman should always defer to the lady.

I should've taken my lessons from Sun Tzu: never apologize because it shows weakness. She took the syrup. I had to wait for it and for her to initiate the conversation, which she did. "When were you going to tell me about Jimmy?"

"I wasn't." She held the dispenser, eyes wide. Taken aback. "Why the hell not?"

"Because we would be having this conversation."

"Because I'm a lawyer?"

"That, and I don't want to jam you up."

She hadn't blinked when she said, "Jam me up?"

"That's what I said."

I started in on my waffles with the heel of my fork.

"You're going to tell me that you were protecting me?"

I enjoyed a sip of coffee before answering. "Yep."

"Those cops were hungry to pin a murder charge on you."

"What can I say? The police and I have history." I crunched a strip of bacon.

She made a tentative inroad into her French toast. She allowed me to watch her take a few bites, for me to watch her clench her jaws. Her tactic was to sit and wait until the proverbial ice cracked or the coffee went cold. I set down my fork, folded my hands over the dish, and stared at her.

"Tell me about this dog," she said.

"A standard poodle named Boo."

She had the mug before her lips. "Any idea whether it is a stud or a bitch?"

"No difference to me. Boo is Jimmy's dog, and that's all that matters."

"Show dog of value, or is Jimmy sentimental?"

"Sentimental," I answered. "Jimmy is a killer, a psychopath, or sociopath, or whatever the shrinks want to call him, but every human being has some residue of humanity, if you're willing to look for it. A pet offers unconditional love and acceptance."

"Kind of like you and Delilah."

"I'm not Jimmy, Bonnie. I don't appreciate the comparison."

"You had Vietnam. Jimmy didn't."

"That's below the belt, Bonnie."

"Is it?" she said. "Whether it's in the name of flag and country or some

141

macho idea of honor and fraternity in the North End, it all ends with a body on the ground."

She pushed her dish away. Bonnie's appetite had made short work of her breakfast. "You could have said no to him, and don't tell me you couldn't, because there's always a choice. Always."

Her eyes were still. Her lips glistened from the sticky syrup.

"Let's go there, Counselor. Let's talk choices, and this in no way constitutes sarcasm, but let's say each choice brings with it consequences, seen and unforeseen."

She interrupted me. "There are consequences for withholding secrets. We've been down this road before, Shane."

"Let's revisit it, Bonnie."

She had found my lockbox of discharge papers and medals. I provided a heavily redacted summary of how I had earned two Bronze Stars with V-device and how my group may or may not have been complicit in atrocities. I refused to be ashamed of my time in Vietnam, but I made it clear to her that war was, by definition, an atrocity. Not long after that trip down Amnesia Lane, she met Hunter, an army buddy whom she'd surmised had done some wet work for the CIA. Bonnie knew, going into our relationship, that I accepted work from Mr. B, a mafia don. Hell, she'd met and partied with Tony Two-Times, and was now tutoring his niece in Latin. I had every right to call bullshit on hypocrisy and compromised integrity.

"Set aside," I said, "the predictable outcome from saying no to Jimmy; set aside whatever ethics you have sworn to uphold as a member of the bar, you've withheld secrets of your own."

She squinted. "What the hell have I held back from you?"

"Duncan's past. He did time in juvie."

"What are you talking about? I told you he had shoplifted."

"You didn't mention the horror show called Shirley."

"It was one sentence in his jacket: You're the PI. You find the facts, and I work the rest."

"Details matter. Context matters. You didn't tell me the kid had a bad foot."

The waitress interrupted and refreshed our coffees. I waited until she'd stepped away.

Bonnie put both elbows on the table and leaned forward. "I didn't know how bad it was until I met the kid. Same for the hand. You were already working the case, and I didn't want you to go into the case biased."

"Biased? Israel Duncan is a black kid. He might as well be the cockroach found swimming inside a bowl of clam chowder. The white kind."

"What is your point?"

"The system maimed him, Bonnie, hand and foot."

"I didn't put two and two together until I met the kid, I swear."

"What they did to him in Shirley is the ace in your pocket. So, Counselor, what are you going to do with it?"

"Get him cleared of this charge first, and then I file a civil suit."

"Bullshit."

My reply had shocked her. She shot back into the upholstered booth. "Why is it bullshit?"

"Because once you win the case, if you win it, the firm will want you to move on. Pro bono is done, and a civil suit is someone else's problem, not to mention that the partners in your firm will not want to take on the Commonwealth and jeopardize their political connections. If the partners at the firm feel magnanimous, they may refer him to another lawyer. The operative word is may, as in the subjunctive."

The waitress took away our dishes. I asked to see a menu.

Bonnie lowered her voice, kept it on autopilot for tone. "Life for Duncan is more complicated than whether the toilet paper goes over or under, Shane."

"Tell me something I don't know."

"He'll be offered a deal. It'll be take it or leave it."

"I know, Bonnie. According to the law, no sane person would plead guilty to a crime he didn't commit, but ask the poor and everyone not white how their trip through the legal system went."

"He refuses, and the DA will have to do his job."

The waitress returned. "What will it be, folks?"

I asked for a frappé and handed her the laminated menu. Bonnie said she was fine. The waitress wrote the order down in her little pad and snuck a look at us as a couple. She must have wondered how Cupid had come to pair us. Bonnie was business professional, put together, and I was weathered, mauled, and wearing the scent of seaweed and seagulls. She pocketed her pad and disappeared.

I asked her, "Do you have a way to make the DA not want to have this go to trial?"

"Do you have any information for me that could help Duncan?"

I said, "I do."

"Is it legal?"

"It's the legal version of a street fight."

The frappé had arrived, a slur of chocolate against the glass and shards of shredded coconut sitting on a cloud of whipped cream. Bonnie peeled off her jacket.

"Let's hear it, but know that any new facts are subject to discovery."

Discovery was legal talk for showing the cards used during the game. Strategy was how each lawyer played his or her hand, if the case went to trial.

If it went to trial.

Between sips of my chocolate drink, I explained to Bonnie that I had visited a certain soda jerk and learned that her client favored cherry sodas. I told her I had a copy of the body search performed on the defendant, but the ruse was to let opposing counsel think this was a gambit at police harassment. That was our bluff.

Bonnie listened to what Noah had dug up on the Armstrong couple. We both agreed that the DA might try to have the payout to the maid made inadmissible. The subtext there was it would save Mrs. Armstrong from public humiliation. I explained that the maid was nowhere to be found.

"Argue an alternate theory of the crime?" Bonnie said.

"If the butler did it in the movies, why not the maid? She had both the means and the opportunity."

I watched her think. The third leg of any crime was motive.

"And what was her motive?" she asked. "She'd already received a payout."

"Greed. Spite. A woman scorned," I answered.

"Not a crime."

144

"But fraud is, and you could put it in the DA's ear that you can prove conspiracy."

"Between Mr. Armstrong and his mistress?"

"I'd argue a threesome. Say the wife knew it, and the argument about saving her from embarrassment goes up in smoke."

Bonnie's eyes registered surprise. I explained the fence, the ticket that was good for sixty days, the money that Mr. Sunglasses behind the counter had fronted to our MIA maid. After I finished the drink with a loud slurp, I mentioned Estrella's address in East Boston, the likelihood of her being an illegal alien, and the possibility she was out of the country.

"But you don't think she left the country?" Bonnie said.

I shook my head. "If it's hard enough to get in, why leave? And don't forget your other ace."

"Excuse me? You said my ace was what happened to Duncan in Shirley."

"Insurance fraud. The Armstrongs are rich in influence, short on cash. You've read enough Austen to know social status and no money is an affliction of the rich."

"So is gout," she said, which made me smile.

"Pitch the idea that the Armstrongs were hard up. Insinuate that they knew the insurance company wouldn't shell out the cash for several months to a year, so they told the maid, 'Here's an advance. Pawn the ring for whatever you can get for it, kick it back to us, and live off what we gave you until it's safe to come in from the cold.'"

"That's a whole lotta trust, Shane, and we can't prove she kicked the money back to them."

"You think any of them filled out a deposit slip at the bank? And you're right, it is a lot of trust, which is why I think the wife was in on it."

"I thought you said the husband was banging the maid."

"Like a screen door in a hurricane, but money trumps poverty any day of the week."

Bonnie thought through the twists and turns of fidelity and greed while I put the empty glass to the side for the waitress.

Bonnie mused. "It is an alternate theory of the crime."

"Whatever theory the DA chases, cutting Duncan loose starts to look attractive."

"And if he doesn't?"

"Drop a dime with the IRS or INS. It's petty, but the phone line to the DA's Office will burn like a fuse on *Mission Impossible* when the Armstrongs start calling in favors. Another option is to tell the DA that you think that the ring has been found at a pawn shop. Say it in front of the aggrieved couple. Whether it's true or not, drop that little bomb and watch what happens between Mr. and Mrs. Armstrong when they realize there is no insurance money."

The waitress left the check at the table's edge. I reached for it, but Bonnie stopped me.

"I changed my mind; my treat." She reached for her purse.

I watched her handle some bills. "Where are you with Andrea and Latin?"

Bonnie explained that the two had established a schedule, now that Bonnie was cleared to visit Tony's mother's house. I inquired more about the matriarch. Bonnie told me that the woman was a character. She explained to me that the granddame so feared poverty for her daughter that she made the down payment on her kid's house and held the deed. She owned the property, not her daughter, not her son-in-law. Her daughter and granddaughter lived with her until the divorce was finalized. Nothing surprised me, and I said as much to Bonnie.

"I could've told you the woman was a piece of work. The way Tony explained it, she's a cross between Lucrezia Borgia and the Tigress of Forlì." The expression on Bonnie's face said she didn't know the second name, so I explained it to her. "Lucrezia poisoned her enemies; Caterina Sforza had them disemboweled."

I got out of the booth. I held her blazer jacket open for her to slip her arms in.

Bonnie let me button her jacket when she turned around.

"There's something that's been bothering me about your second run-in with the police."

I fixed her scarf. "Why the cops thought I was there?"

"I'm thinking Jimmy has someone inside the police department."

Chapter Twenty-Four: At the Office

Bonnie let me borrow her car after I dropped her off at work. I decided to enter the enemy's country, the part of Boston that Nick Carraway from Middle America would never have described in rhapsodic language. Jimmy was no Jay Gatsby, but he lived in Southie.

Across the street from me was a liquor store, his unofficial office. It was a dull concrete box with plate glass for a window looking out to the street. The corrugated metal security frontage had been rolled up to signal Open For Business. A man in a white bowling shirt, a flat cap on his head and an unlit stogie in his mouth, manned the register. A simple sign over the entrance promised Free Deliveries. There was a big parking lot for a front yard and a large shamrock painted on a sidewall. Jimmy's black Mercury Grand Marquis was parked, neat and perfect, between the only two white lines in the lot. An unexpected fog from the nearby beaches gave Old Colony Avenue the kind of shroud that would have delighted Jack the Ripper.

Booze and cigarettes. Jimmy controlled both from an office in the back. This was where we had first met. The rumor goes that Jimmy needed a legitimate front, so he offered the previous owners a handsome amount of money to the husband of the couple that owned the place, enough for him and the missus to do the one-way ticket to Florida. The husband agreed to the amount and the sale. His wife did not. She sent hubby back to renege on the agreement.

He never came home.

She disappeared.

I walked in and ignored the "Hey! Can I help you?" from the man at the front desk.

The place was a sty, opened boxes, unopened boxes everywhere. Wine bottles were in disarray, not racked by region, varietal, or price. Beers were accorded even less respect and organization. Ales, lagers, and stouts, Irish in one section, British in another. Grannies had their own section for hard cider. Hard liquor was organized behind the counter with the cigarettes.

As I expected, Jimmy placed a sentry in front of the flap doors to his office. A scrawny kid who fancied himself as a member of Notre Dame's Fighting Irish blocked the doorway. He smiled with a set of bad teeth in a pasty face. The grin wouldn't stop me. He put his hand forward in a feeble attempt to stop. I twisted it and bent the fingers back with my left hand until there was an awful crunch. I didn't care for his scream, so I punched him with a right hook to the side of the head. He fell. I stepped over him.

A small lamp glowed in the distance. Jimmy sat in a chair behind a desk. There was a chair in front of me. I dragged it slowly enough for the legs to scrape the concrete floor. The scent of mildew that I associated with body bags in the service permeated the air. Behind the desk, Jimmy's torso looked as if it were shrink-wrapped in a white muscle shirt. Not a set of weights in sight, but he looked pumped from a compound set of bench presses and triceps extensions. His biceps bulged. I could count the veins in his neck. The glare from the lamp cast him as an albino with royal eyes.

"The cops came for me," I said.

Jimmy held up two fingers. "Twice."

He pulled open the middle drawer. He placed a .38 on the naked wood.

I pointed to his piece on the desk. "Used it to kill Seamus?"

"Could be."

The revolver on the wood didn't seem personalized in any way. Guys on the force made small touches. When I carried, mine conformed to departmental regulations like an office man in a gray flannel suit.

I nodded to the gun in front of him. "I'm getting déjà vu looking at it."

"Because it looks familiar?"

"It does."

"It should because it's yours."

"What are the odds?" I said. "Is it sheer coincidence that you, of all people, ended up with an ex-cop's service revolver?"

"It's not, and I'll explain if you're interested."

"I'm very interested."

I was intent, focused. Time stretched elastic, and I counted every mote of dust in the air.

"I didn't know the gun was yours until after the fact. God's honest truth," he said, right hand raised before he lowered it.

"Explain how you came by my service revolver."

He grinned. "I think you know the answer to that question. If not, you're the detective."

"Private investigator. There's a difference," I said. "Please answer the question."

"The BPD should've had the .38 designated for destruction, but that didn't happen because you have so many friends in the department. Someone kept it for a rainy day."

"Still haven't answered the damn question, Jimmy."

"My number-two man gave me the piece. You'll notice he isn't here."

"I noticed. The featherweight outside your door will need to have his fingers splinted."

Jim cocked his head back for a good laugh.

"I'll buy him a beer as a Band-Aid."

"Back to the gun, Jimmy."

"You and I need to get this beyond us. I hope that's possible."

"Looks like, feels like a frame, Jimmy, and it reeks of your special friend."

"I wasn't trying to drop you into the tank with the sharks, I swear."

He did have expressive eyes. Like Newman's.

I told him, "I'm thinking your Number Two acted as the deliveryman for your friend."

"Plausible theory."

"Thing is, Jimmy, he owns you, and we both know it. You're Number Two, and it is likely his eyes and ears on you. Agree?"

"Not your problem, Shane Cleary."

"So you're looking out for me, is that it?"

"They find a body to match the weapons?" His eyes looked to the revolver.

"I can't imagine your friend is happy with you."

"I want my dog back, that's all."

His guardian angel had tried to transform me into a metal cube, courtesy of a car compactor in Somerville. To his credit, Jimmy tried to intervene and save me then, but John was the boss, the master. Jimmy was his boy, his puppet, and John controlled the strings.

He came out with it. "John didn't know I'd hired you."

The words shot out of my mouth. "He does now," I said. "He hands you that .38, so the cops think I killed Seamus Costigan." I pointed to the weapon. "Problem for me is they won't let it go. How unfortunate for me. Problem for you is Seamus has a brother, and he'll come for you."

"I'll take care of it."

I wasn't expecting an apology. On paper, there wasn't much of a case against me. No body. No bullet. That was the extent to which Jimmy made good on the trouble he had created for me for taking the case, for finding his dog. All the cops had to show for evidence were footprints from work boots. Hundreds of guys who worked construction were viable suspects.

"Any news on Boo?"

The voice was the sound of a child hidden inside the body of an adult. Boo was his world.

"Malcolm, the dog groomer," I said. "The kid had nothing to do with Boo's disappearance. The Costigan brothers were two Southie dots who destroyed his livelihood. The kid is living in fear because he's afraid of retaliation for his mistake."

"And you think I should do something about that?"

"The Costigan brothers walked into the place acting as if they were part of your crew."

"They shouldn't have done that."

"Doesn't stop wannabees from saying they're connected or made guys, but it happens."

"What do you suggest I do?" Jimmy asked.

"Same thing I told the brothers, leave an envelope in the kid's mailbox. They're the ones who took Boo and then lost him." I stood up, stopped, and said to Jimmy. "Take care of the problem in your backyard, or someone else will."

Jimmy smiled. "Might that person be Shane Cleary?"

I shook my head. "No, but now that I think about it. Dim and Dimmer shook down a bar in Central Square, and people may think they did it with your blessing and that you're taking a cut of the action. That's unhealthy for them and unhealthy for you. On that note, I'm outta here."

I walked out into the mess of the world. Nothing had changed. The boxes were still there, unpacked. The manager's cigar was still unlit. There was the crying kid, who had thought he was tough, but wasn't. When he grows up, he'll learn to hide his pain, like the rest of us.

Chapter Twenty-Five: The Duel

This country has been divided about many things, but its citizens have never wavered about how much they hate lawyers, and yet, I was opposite one in a car, about to join one in a meeting with Suffolk County's District Attorney.

The DA had asked Bonnie to meet him at Post Office Square. She played meek and mild over the phone. She told me he would dictate terms. All part of the game, and she said it with a laugh straight out of the archives for the femme fatale. The subtext was she hadn't rated the professional courtesy of a negotiation in his office at Bulfinch Place.

"Maybe he has a case in the McCormack Courthouse?"

"Nothing between lawyers is casual, Shane. Everything is strategic. Everything."

The expression on Bonnie's face was a combo of pity and scorn, as in I should have known better. I had asked an ingénue's question. I was told to play my part. She was the star, and I was a supporting actor.

The John W. McCormack U.S. Post Office and Courthouse adjudicated bankruptcies on the fifth floor aired federal cases on the third floor, and the rest of the structure was office spaces and, of course, a post office. His Lord Highness asked to meet us here as if he was on his way to mail some letters.

Bonnie took the keys out of the ignition and dropped them into her purse. Two shades of blue, eyeliner and shadow, complimented her eyes. Lips were done in a shade of red I had neither seen nor enjoyed before. I couldn't take my eyes off her. She checked her face in the mirror.

"Different lipstick, so he'll pay attention to what I'm saying." She grinned.

"You men can't hold a train of thought before it derails and visits the gutter. Too bad for most women, the ride doesn't last long."

"Thanks for the compliment. You think he'll last long?"

"I didn't include you when I said 'you men.'"

"Aside from the massive generalization, why do I oddly feel as if I've been complimented and emasculated at the same time."

She opened her door, looked over her shoulder at me, and said, "Men are the sensitive gender."

We walked down Milk Street through the vanguard of the Finance District. From offices, lone individuals ran out for quick coffees or fast cigarette breaks, their minds busy with whatever they did between then and lunch or plotting how they'd spend that next paycheck.

Soon enough, we were at one of the multiple entrances to the courthouse. Art Deco and Moderne were atypical for government buildings built during the Depression. LA's City Hall was one other notable exception. Bonnie informed me the meeting was in a research room adjacent to the law library. He had reserved the room, she said, to emphasize his display of power. A reservation implied a time limit, a need for her to press his case into either coal or diamonds. I was listening as I took in the measure of the architectural monstrosity. There were walls clad in New England granites, terracotta relief patterns, metal grilles, and marble accents.

We rode the Otis up. The sound of the bell and the elevator doors closing marked us as stupid, brave, or both. The elevator opened out to a quiet foyer. I began to understand and appreciate Bonnie's line of work. All this silence was a prelude to an ambush. I was familiar with that sensation. I felt as if I was back in Vietnam, on patrol. We all knew Charlie was in the bush. Bonnie had agreed to meet the enemy on his terms, on the territory of his choosing. Bonnie came to the field for the duel.

The District Attorney introduced himself and his second man.

"So glad we can meet. Bonnie, this is Mr. Thomas, my assistant."

"Thank you for meeting me, Edward. This is my research associate, Shane Cleary."

I went with the flow. After I shook hands with the DA and his assistant, the DA indicated the way to a table and chairs for two, a clock on the wall, and the slightest of windows. The room was large enough to remind an aristocrat that he was still a prisoner in the Tower of London.

Mr. Thomas stood behind the DA, and I stood behind Bonnie. There was no third party to spell out the rules of combat. Whoever spoke first would decide on sword or pistol. He offered a wide, toothy grin above his bowtie, folded hands, and manicured fingernails on the table.

The DA said, "Have you and your client reconsidered the plea deal?"

"He has, and the answer is no." She said it hard, fast, and with certainty. "I'm offering you the opportunity to drop the case and save yourself and The Commonwealth the scandal, not to mention the embarrassment that this case will cause the Armstrong family."

For a second, the DA's face dropped and paled. Her words, his reaction, revealed that he hadn't worn a cup to the match. As I had expected, his wolfish grin reappeared. He glanced over his shoulder. He and Thomas shared a complicit laugh.

"Bold words, Bonnie, but you haven't a pot to piss in, and you know it. The thing about you women lawyers is you think you have to have brass balls like the boys in the club."

"But it is a club, Edward. Rather than think of it as bombast, I'd prefer you accept my terms as a gift, as an act of mercy."

"I see," he said. "This wouldn't be some form of payback for our little affair during law school, would it?" He directed his next comment to me. "I was a junior at Harvard Law, and she was at Suffolk."

I couldn't resist. "I'm amazed she had time to slum since she worked full-time."

Edward flexed a forced smile and turned his attention to her. "You don't have the stamina to go all twelve rounds in the courtroom with me, our past notwithstanding."

"There's a recurring male fantasy for you. Stamina"

"There is another one," he said. "It's called I win, and you lose."

Bonnie folded her hands. "Edward, you were a mercy fuck then, and this is an act of compassion now. Our personal history aside, this case could ruin your career. As a colleague, I'd advise you to drop the case."

"I have to uphold the office—"

"You mean save face or your pride? Let's look at the facts, shall we?"

Mr. Thomas, the researcher, put his hand into the fray. "Your client has a history of theft."

"As a child, and that hardly constitutes a career criminal. The evidence in your case does not hold up to scrutiny."

Bonnie lifted up her briefcase. She pressed the release on the brass plates, and flaps popped. She reached in and pulled out a folder. She placed sheets of paper in front of the DA. His assistant stepped forward to have a look over his shoulder.

"This document is ancient history," the DA said.

Bonnie pointed at it. "Open the door to his prior as a child, and that piece of paper will grind your career to a halt, and let me remind you, it's germane to the case because it obliterates your timeline."

"What timeline?" Edward looked at it, puzzled. "What the hell are you talking about?"

"That's the point, Edward. That piece of paper in front of you is about Cottage Nine in Shirley. It's where kids were abused. It's all there, in graphic detail, Edward. Israel Duncan sustained serious injuries to his right hand and foot. He never received medical treatment for them. Trust me, neither the Commonwealth nor your office wants Cottage Nine in the news."

Edward's eyes moved from one sheet to the next. "This is your backdoor out of the case?"

"No, it's evidence, Edward. You still run along the Charles River?"

Suspicious, his eyes narrowed. "When I have the time. Why?"

"Seven-minute mile, if I recall. Imagine you had a foot like Israel Duncan. Now imagine how long it would take you to hobble from the Armstrong residence to this soda fountain, which Mr. Cleary investigated for me."

Bonnie handed him detailed notes I had typed up for her.

"I have yet to introduce this into discovery," she said. "The proprietor of that shop helps establish a timeline, a pattern even, because the kid came into his shop on a regular basis before visiting his aunt at MGH. Want more?"

Bonnie extracted more paperwork from her briefcase. She looked at Thomas. "I'll skip over the fact that Duncan would've had one hell of a time breaking and entering with his mangled hand. Say what you will about his left hand, and postulate all you want that he disposed of the screwdriver the police claimed he had used on the door. Fact is no screwdriver was ever found." She shoved the police analysis report on the door in front of him. "Insist on the B&E, and I'll show there was no way that Israel Duncan could have done that kind of damage to the door and lock left-handed. Now, let us look at the cavity search document here."

Bonnie handed that document to him. She gave the two men a few seconds to scan it.

Edward tossed the paper at her. "Nice try, Counselor. Shake that pretty blonde head all you want, but a jury won't buy your innuendo that this was racist. You can say the body search was police harassment, and I'll say they were looking for the ring."

"Harvard Law and all, and you still don't get it. I'll let Mr. Cleary explain it to you."

"Explain what?"

I picked up the sheet he had flung at her and planted it in front of him. My finger pointed to the box. "Read what is typed in that box."

"'Tongue: Cherry.' So what?"

"You forgot to mention that the officer check marked the box for 'Abnormal' instead of 'Normal.' Why is this important, you may ask, and I'll tell you. Because the kid has a fondness for cherry sodas. You could say Duncan had all the time in the world to break into the Armstrong home, steal a valuable ring, and order a fountain soda, and visit his aunt at MGH on time, despite the limp and the damaged claw. You decide whether or not you tell the jury that the nurses gave depositions that he had never once arrived late."

I paused for effect.

"All these details underscore the fact that the two patrolmen never filed a report that they had spoken to the owner of that convenience shop. Imagine how incompetence will sit with the jury."

The DA handed the form to Thomas without looking at him. Edward drummed his fingers on the table. He had assumed she was done. He twisted his lips as if he'd swallowed postnasal drip. He huffed.

"I'll consider a lesser charge. Damage to private property. What do you say?"

Bonnie snapped the buckle shut on her briefcase. Handsome and expensive leather, something her parents had saved up to buy for her as a graduation gift. Bonnie had been the first in her family to attend college, the first to acquire a profession.

"What I have to say, I won't because I'm a lady," she answered. "Drop the case. Israel Duncan walks."

"Don't be absurd," Edward said. "The ring is still unaccounted for."

"About that ring," Bonnie said.

Edward raised his hand. "I know what you are going to say. You're going to say that you have an alternate theory of the crime. We know about the maid, about the money, the affair, and you can argue that she may have stolen the damn ring and—"

"But you agreed to spare Mrs. Armstrong the humiliation. How charitable of you."

He shook his head. "This could backfire on you. A jury could be sympathetic."

"You want to take that chance? Let me save you some time and give you something to chew on, Edward. I can flip the story and say that Mrs. Armstrong and her maid were having a torrid affair."

"The implication is that they were all in on it together, is that it?"

"I'd love to see how that flies and lands. What was her name, Shane?"

"Estrella Esperanza."

"You're right. A jury may sympathize." Bonnie's hand wobbled like a seesaw. "Maybe or maybe not. Maybe when we have the couple and the maid together in one room, one of them flips. But there's one problem, isn't there, Edward?"

"No ring," he said.

"There's that, but there's another matter. You're wrong."

"Wrong about what?"

"I'm thinking back to when a certain law student explained to another student what a good narrative can do or how juries like to see the bigger picture. The law is not all about what you can prove, but what you can make people think happened." She turned to me. "Imagine that, Suffolk teaching Harvard."

I shrugged. "The lesson didn't stick. Apparently."

Bonnie gathered the papers on the table into a stack. She pushed them in front of the DA.

"You keep those," she said. "Mr. Cleary here confirmed for me that insurance companies don't pay out big money right away. Six months, isn't that right, Mr. Cleary?"

"Sometimes a year."

She tapped the top page on the stack. Edward wasn't looking so hale.

"Run with your narrative, Edward. Say the master of the house was banging the maid, paid her off, and I'll propose my own theory that the couple hired the maid and paid her to disappear with the ring, but she walked off with it."

"You're suggesting a double-cross, which you can't prove because there's no maid." He grinned. "The big picture, as you so put it."

Bonnie pushed her chair back. She stood up.

"Here's your big picture, Eddie. The Armstrong couple spots a black kid walking past their house several times a week. They blame it on him. Between the Hispanic maid and the black kid, they relied on racial stereotypes, which in today's climate is like holding a lit firecracker. Save time, avoid publicity, and keep the very important people happy. I wouldn't be surprised if someone made a call and the insurance company cuts a check post haste."

"You can't prove a thing."

"I don't have to," she said. "Mr. Cleary reminded me that the law is the law, but when it comes to the courtroom, juries often don't understand the law. What did you call it, Mr. Cleary?

"Perception."

The DA had that worried look. He blinked more than once.

"Squeeze the Armstrong couple yourself and see what they say," she said. "You could avoid a boatload of grief that way, or one of us could call the IRS and INS and see what comes up in the wash."

I pushed in her chair. Bonnie was prepared for a grand exit.

Edward's rise from the table was half statesman, having signed the treaty, and half spoiled brat who wanted the last word. He wasn't going down without a retort. I hadn't forgotten his dig directed at me that he had known Bonnie in the biblical sense while they were law students.

"So you two worked together on this case," he said, somewhat amused by the idea. "The same Shane Cleary, who was suspected of a murder recently. Oh yeah, no body. *Corpus delicti.*" He smirked at Bonnie. "I heard that you're his counsel. As for perception, the jury would love to hear all about Mr. Cleary and you when he's on the stand. Should I call him to testify about this soda jerk and cherry sodas?" Edward looked at me as if I had sneezed into his hand. "The same Cleary who ratted on cops, whose father blew his brains out."

He'd intended to get a rise out of me. I was tempted. I stepped forward, forcing him to peddle backwards. I reached over and straightened his bowtie. "You wouldn't want to go down that road, Counselor."

"And what road might that might be?"

"Make sure when you call me to the stand the jury understands that this case was pro bono, and I wasn't paid a dime by Ms. Loring or her firm. Ever read Sherlock Holmes, Counselor?"

That had thrown him, and his face registered confusion.

"I have, but I don't see the relevance here."

"Doyle said cops were 'Brave as a bulldog and as tenacious as a lobster if he gets his claws upon anyone.' I don't think of myself as a bulldog, but he's right about the lobster. I'm tenacious."

Bonnie was quiet in the elevator. I could tell that she was reviewing her performance. I doubted she worried about me and my reaction to the unnecessary disclosure Edward had made earlier. It was a cheap shot, unprofessional.

I said, "You took my advice about the bluff."

Her eyes looked sideways at me, a smile formed on those nice red lips of hers. The doors parted, and I said, "Lady first, and I need to find a payphone." She looked at me, and I said, "I need to follow up with Delano. He'll have a name and an address for me."

Chapter Twenty-Six: The Big Lie

The exterior of a house says volumes about the people inside. A certain decal in the window alerts the fireman to a child's room. A flag on the porch proclaims patriotism and implies military service. Chairs on the porch suggested folks watched the street and talked through the summer's nights. The car's model and year implied income. Cracked sidewalks hinted at neglect and a lackadaisical attitude toward maintenance. The five digits of the zip code were all shorthand for the high and low, the Haves and Have-Nots. In my South End, everyone lived the hardcore blue-collar life. We were working-class stiffs who were stiffed because we worked hard.

I searched lawns for a splotch of crab grass, a chorus of dandelions. Grass invited the lifted leg, the undignified squat of man's best friend. Lindsey had typed up a list of names and addresses of all the delivery boys. The newsies knew who had dogs on their routes. If Boo had escaped from the Costigan brothers, he wouldn't have strayed too far from where they lived in Somerville, which explained why Jimmy couldn't find his dog in Southie or around Malcolm's place in Roxbury.

I sat inside Bonnie's car and cased one house in Somerville. Nice yard inside an enclosure of chain-link fencing so fresh the diamond pattern hadn't rusted or sagged yet. The owners had invested in a quality hedge, sure to outlast most marriages. I consulted the information that the Professor conveyed over the phone. The kid's name was Nicky. I was betting that the dog, the big black poodle he was playing with, was Boo. I cracked the window so I could listen to the boy and his dog.

The dog kid called the dog Charlie. The way this dog acted convinced me that I'd laid eyes on the right canine. Charlie studied people. He listened before he acted. When he moved, he bounded with energy, grace, and vigor. If poodles were divas, Charlie was nothing like that. He matched Nicky for energy and rambunctious spirit.

Which made my decision painful and difficult because the inevitable amounted to taking a child's Christmas toy away from him or worse, handing it to another kid in front of him.

Bonnie's car now parked and locked, I walked the half-block to a payphone, dropped a dime, and dialed the number to the liquor store. Nicky and Charlie continued to cavort on their lawn. Nicky shouted some command, and the dog dropped down to roll left, roll right several times. He sprung up to attention and awaited the next call in agility exercises.

"Yo," the voice answered the phone.

"Nice way to answer the phone."

"Who the fuck is this?"

"The guy who broke your fingers. Put Jimmy on the phone."

"Doncha know the word 'please'?" he said in typical Southie brogue. He had left his ah in 'doncha' as open as his fly. "What makes you think he'll take your call?"

"Listen, kid," I said. "Put him on, or when I see him next and tell him you hung up on me, your boss will do more than break your other hand."

"What should I tell him?"

"One word: Boo."

"Are you joking?"

"Do I sound like it?"

"Hold on."

He dropped the handset, and it must've banged against the wall because it clanged in my ear. Spiteful brat. A moment later, there's the scuffle of loud and louder footsteps, and then voices: Jimmy's and the kid's. I could picture Jimmy putting the phone to his ear. His bright blues would have blinked once or twice before he spoke.

"This is Jim."

"Cleary here. Got pen and paper? I'm at this address."

I gave Jimmy the location. He either wrote it down or committed it to memory.

"Boo is there?"

"His name is Charlie now, and yes, he's here. I'm looking at him as I speak."

"Some low-life snatched him?"

"Little kid named Nicky, and I wouldn't say low-life. Nice family, nice house, and nice life. My guess is the kid found the dog and adopted him."

"I'll be there in a few."

I hung up. My hand was still on the blue handset. I'd done what I'd been hired to do. I'd found the dog Boo. Jimmy would arrive soon, if he broke several traffic laws in transit. I was convinced that Nicky and his parents had no idea who owned Charlie. The kid found the dog, or the dog had found him in the streets. Like a scene from *Leave It to Beaver*, Nicky had come home, begged, and pleaded with his parents to keep the dog. He promised he'd groom it, walk it, and clean up after it. There was another reason why I was hundred percent certain that Charlie was Boo.

When Jimmy had hired me, he told me that Boo had a certain collar and no tags. Nicky's parents, seeing no tags, ID, or flyers for a missing dog in the neighborhood, adopted the dog and didn't swap out the collar. There was no need to. I don't know how they had come up with the name Charlie. My guesses wandered everywhere from Southeast Asia, to a Steinbeck novel about a road trip across America, to the extreme possibility that Charlie was Charlie Brown. I headed to Bonnie's car for the sit and wait.

The black Mercury Grand Marquis slid into a parking space behind me twenty minutes later. Jimmy alone and wearing sunglasses. He got out of the car. I opened my door and put a leg out. The house, Nicky, and the dog were across the street. I said I wanted a word.

"What is it?"

I pointed to the house. "If you plan to get violent, I walk. I want no part of it."

"Nothing will happen. All I want is my dog."

Jimmy led the way across the street. He lifted the hook and pushed in the gate. I turned to close it behind us. Nicky stopped playing. The dog didn't bark, but he sniffed the air, hesitant in his approach to Jimmy. He lowered his head, eyes intent on Jimmy. Jimmy crouched down eye-to-eye with the poodle. The dog broke out in a happy dance, head and front paws bobbing up and down before he rushed Jimmy, who hugged him. I doubted that Jimmy had ever hugged anyone other than his mother and father, and that was a big maybe. The screen door creaked. Nicky's parents had ambled out onto the porch. The expression on their faces was not of sadness for their kid and his dog, but of quiet terror of being in Jimmy's presence.

"He's your dog, isn't he, mister?" Nicky asked.

"Afraid so. Can we go inside and talk?"

We followed Nicky to the threshold, where he stood next to his parents.

Jimmy took off the sunglasses. "Do you know who I am?" he asked the father.

The aroma of a nice dinner was in the air around the all-American family. The wife forced a smile.

Jim said to her, "May I come inside?"

The couple looked at each other. The father stepped aside after Jimmy wiped his feet on the welcome mat. He introduced me as the PI he had hired to find the missing dog. He told them Charlie's real name was Boo and how he appreciated that they had taken such good care of his dog. Jimmy reached into his jacket. The father stepped back.

"A little something for your trouble." Jimmy wiggled a fat envelope in his hand. "Please, take it. I insist."

The father's shaky hand accepted the parcel. He didn't look at it or inside it. He handed it to his wife. Jimmy suggested that they put his gratitude to good use, on their lovely home or to set up a college fund for Nicky. "May I have a word with your son before I leave?" he asked the husband. The man mumbled as if his mouth were dry. Jimmy kept a straight face. His blue eyes looked through you more than at you.

The mother stood fixed, frozen. She was slight, an apron tied around her waist, plain features, and a Dorothy Hamill wedge cut. He was in from some office somewhere in brown slacks, bruised Oxfords, regulation white shirt, and bland tie, the knot pulled down the second he had left the building. Decent people. Ordinary people.

Jimmy hinged forward like an umpire behind home plate and leveled his eyes at the kid.

"Nicky, right?"

The kid looked to his mother for permission. She lifted her chin.

"Yes, sir. Nicholas is my name, though my friends call me Nicky."

Jimmy put out his hand. The kid took it tentatively. They shook hands as Jimmy spoke.

"I can't say that I have many friends, but I'd like to think you and I can be friends. Call me Jim or Jimmy. I appreciate you looking after Charlie. Thank you. Can I ask you something? And be honest with me, Nicky."

The boy nodded, his eyes perhaps fixated on Jim's remarkable eyes. "Sure," he said.

"Know who I am?"

The kid nodded.

"I'm sure what people say about me is not nice."

The kid didn't answer.

"Tell me, Nicky, what does your dad do for a living?"

"Accountant. He's an accountant."

The kid swallowed hard when Jimmy leaned down behind him and put his lips near the boy's left ear. He might have done the same thing to Seamus in the chair out there in that shack. Lean down and whisper into the man's ear, the poor bastard's heart beating faster than a hummingbird's wings.

"Look at your dad, Nicky."

The kid did, and I didn't know what to expect from Jimmy.

"There's an honest man for you, the kind of man you should become. Understand? I know what people say about me, but that's okay. I'm not like your father, Nicky, and do you know why?" Jim paused. "Because I don't have many friends, which is why Charlie means so much to me. He doesn't judge me. I don't expect you to understand that, Nicky, but Charlie is the only friend I have, which is why I want him back."

The kid turned around. "You promise to take care of him?"

166

"I promise."

"Promise he'll get a lot of exercise?"

"I promise."

"Protect him, so nothing bad will happen to him."

"I promise."

The kid embraced Jimmy. For a second, Jimmy smiled, and his hand stroked the kid's hair.

Outside, Jimmy asked me to follow him to the liquor store. He wanted to pay me, he said, and I was all too happy to conclude our business.

Boo sat in the front seat of the Marquis. Had the dog not moved now and then, I would've thought it was a woman with a tight perm in the passenger seat. Jimmy drove within the speed limit. He obeyed the lights. His head moved, not to look both ways, but to talk to Boo. His right hand lifted for the occasional caress.

He parked his car in his regular spot. I eased Bonnie's car next to his. I saw the kid with the damaged hand through the glass to the Liquor-Mart in front of us. I exited the car and waited as Jimmy walked around his vehicle to open the door for the dog.

I followed the two of them into the store, through the minefield of crates, into the back office. Boo sauntered, nails clicking on the concrete in the darkened office.

"Sit," Jim said.

"Me or the dog?"

"You. That chair there, and turn on the light."

To use the word 'please' was a sign of weakness to Jimmy. I pulled the beaded chain, and the office lamp came to life. Boo was curled up in a bed on the floor. Jimmy worked the dial to his safe and pulled a lever. The door groaned open.

"I never asked," I said. "Is Boo a he or a she?"

"A she. You'd know if you checked the undercarriage."

Jimmy placed a stack of bills on the desk. "Sorry I couldn't gift wrap it for you."

He sat down in his chair, and I let the money sit there. I didn't want to look greedy or desperate. I thanked him, and he asked me, "Are we good?"

"There's the personal detail. Remember?" I allowed the question to hang in the air.

"Right," Jimmy said. "Our agreement. You take the gig, and I'd tell you something you didn't know about your father."

"That was the deal, yes."

"I'm many things, Shane Cleary, but I do keep my word." Jim's face was a white mask in the lamp's glare, the blueness of his eyes pronounced. "Tell me what you remember about your old man."

"What's there to tell?" I said. "He was good and decent, a great father, but not without his own problems. He returned from the war, damaged, like you said. He'd been in Guadalcanal. He never talked about it, but I've met vets who fought there. He said what you remembered most is the grass."

"Grass?" Jimmy said.

"What the Japanese called blood grass. Razor-sharp. Poetic, I thought, when he said it. My father served in Korea, too."

"Seems like he couldn't get enough of it, huh?"

"Or he didn't know what to do with himself. I can relate to that feeling."

"You served in Vietnam," Jimmy said. "Come back damaged like him?"

I never liked talking about myself, about my time in the service, especially, nor did I relish this criminal having any leverage on me. Jimmy hadn't blinked. He knew what I was thinking.

"I'll make this easier for you, Shane. Your father came back from the war shaken and stirred. No shame in that. Most men of his era didn't talk about what they had seen or done. You're the same way. Came home, bottled it up, assuming you don't hit the same bottle. Take up the GI Bill for an education and a better shot at making a living. It kind of reminds me of Nicky's dad."

"How do you figure?" I asked.

"Be a good dad. Hold your little girl's hand to cross the street, or take your boy into the backyard and toss the football or baseball around. Did your dad do that…throw the ball around? Mine did. That one-armed son of a bitch had heart, and I loved him for it. Of course, I had to hold back on how I

168

threw the ball to him."

I wanted to take the money and leave.

"Is there a point to all of this?"

"There is, Shane. There is. Your old man may not have talked about the war, but he did talk about other things. You know, I can't get Al Capone out of my head. He fought in World War One. Did you know that?"

"I did not."

I pictured Boo as Charlie and thought of Jimmy as Charlie Brown's teacher. All noise and no sense to what I was hearing, but I stayed the course and listened.

"You know he had brothers and sisters."

"Al Capone?"

"One of his brothers, Vincenzo, changed his name and became a law officer named Richard 'Two Gun' Hart. He wore a white ten-gallon hat. Al and his brothers called him Jimmy."

I stopped him. "I'm not sure where this train is headed, but I'll go along for the ride if you get to the point soon." I fell back into the chair. I tried not to show attitude, but I was impatient as a schoolkid whose eyes watched the second hand on the clock for the last bell of the school day.

"Okay, I will," he said. "Tell me what you remember about your father's suicide."

"What do you want to know?" I leaned forward and stared right into him. "And why?"

"There's a reason. Trust me."

"Trust you?"

"I helped you. I called your girlfriend the lawyer, didn't I?"

"And you moved a body, so thank you," I told him.

"Tell me what you remember."

I never thought about my father's death, except on the anniversary or on his birthday when I noted how old he would have been had he lived. Hard and human not to do those things.

"He'd been moping around the house days before."

"Depressed?" Jimmy asked.

"No, more like he was preoccupied. My mother and I, well, we soft-stepped around him when he was in a mood. You could see it in his face. You'd know when it came over him. It was unmistakable. He used to have these terrible nightmares about the war, and he'd stay up nights, days at a time, worried about the men he worked with, so I thought that was the case at the time."

My voice had caught. My eyes clouded. All these years, and it still got to me.

"And on the day of?"

"Christ, you don't let up, do you? I was getting to that. My mother and I were out when he did it...in the, in the living room. I was the one who found him. My mother was in the hallway with the grocery bags when I discovered the body. I turned tail to prevent her from seeing him like that, but she did. It was unavoidable, and mind you that all of this happened during the holiday season, between Christmas and New Year. Those days, the stretch between the two holidays, are the worst for me. We'd lost Kennedy and...."

To his credit, Jimmy didn't judge me when my voice trembled. His face maintained the neutral gaze of an officer who'd seen his men dead and stacked like a cord of wood in body bags on the bird home. I had no shame. He was my father. I was fifteen, and the most scandalous thing I should have seen at that age was the flash of a girl's thigh or a bra strap. Not that. Not him, and not like that.

"Do you remember anything else from that morning?"

I looked up, confused. "What are you, a therapist? You want to do hypnosis?"

"You saw him. What happened afterwards?"

Boo had lifted her head and then lowered it.

"Afterwards?" I said. "Afterwards, my mother was inconsolable. We moved soon after. She couldn't live there anymore. Too many memories haunted her. Neither of us could live there anymore. I had to leave school because we couldn't afford it. She died of a broken heart two years later. She dropped dead in an aisle at Purity Supreme. I joined the military not long after." I stopped. "Wait. This I remember. Not long after my father's body was, you know, removed, a group of ladies who knew my parents came in and washed the wall and rug because of the…"

Jimmy had pulled a drawer open. He set out two short glasses and a bottle. There were sounds of a twist and the hollowed plunk of the cork being pulled out. He poured a generous amount of whiskey. Midleton Dair Ghaelach. Expensive stuff.

"I thought you didn't drink."

"I don't," Jimmy said. "This is an exception."

"Hardly in the mood."

"Drink. It's not a request. You'll need it."

I took the glass. He took his. We raised them. *Sláinte.*

The whiskey was complex, creamy against the palate, delicious.

"I told you my old man had an accident," Jimmy said.

"The arm. Railroad cars."

"He scrambled about town, from job to job, taking whatever job he could. One of those jobs was with a construction company. What did your father do for a living, Shane?"

"Construction. Foreman."

"Union man?" Jimmy asked.

"He was a rep, yes, and proud of it. Why?"

"Hold onto that thought," Jimmy said. "My old man clerked at the same construction company where your dad worked. He wasn't there long, but long enough to hear things." He turned the glass in his hand as he recalled the memory. "The feds waste time and money with bugs and all that James Bond surveillance shit when they ought to talk to the secretaries. Want to know the skinny of any office? Talk to the broads at the front desk, my father told me. He said, 'Those dames knew everything, down to the last time the light bulb and Mary Jo in Payables got screwed.' My father learned who was paying whom to build what, where, and when. He had the inside lane on all the union problems and the ways management worked around them. There was this one project—a colossal turd. If there ever was ever one, it stunk. Unsafe didn't cover it. Everybody knew it was a money grab, but nobody said a damn word, except for one person. Guess who had to play Cassandra?"

"A certain foreman?"

Jimmy lifted the bottle and offered. I declined. He poured himself a nip. "We all know what happened to Cassandra from Greek mythology. She told the honest truth, and the Greeks pitched her over the side of a cliff. You know, most people live their entire lives and never know the truth about themselves or life itself. When they hear it, they deny it, because the truth compels them to action. They may discover the truth at the last second before the lights go out when they can't do a damn thing about it, which is why people are screaming for more time at the very end before it's lights out. What would Shane Cleary do if he learned that his life was predicated on a lie? Would he want to hear the truth?"

He asked me to give my answer, so I did. "Yes."

"The big lie is your father's suicide."

"Not suicide?"

"Not if there were two men in the room to make sure he pulled the trigger."

I shot back the whiskey. I've seen the dead, in the military and on the beat. Bodies blown apart, unrecognizable from all kinds of violence. People tortured to death. Kids and old ladies napalmed. I've seen the blade applied with precision, the life gone in a flash of light behind the eyes, and I've seen all ages hacked to death in a frenzy. I learned to live with all of that, but I never forgot the sight of my father in the living room. Every detail. No matter how much I wish I could erase the image from my memory, I can't.

"Someone forced him and then staged the scene?" I asked.

"Worse," Jim said. He poured me some whiskey.

"What could be worse?" I asked.

Jimmy encouraged me with a nod. I drank the rest of the shot.

Jimmy explained. "My father told me the company needed the work, the money. Your father had voiced his concerns about workplace safety. My dad said your father was an effective leader. The men loved him, and they would follow him anywhere and do what he said, which is what management and the finance men feared. He sure as hell wasn't going to jeopardize his men on some half-ass worksite. Management made some concessions at first, but it deteriorated into intimidation tactics. A strike was one thing, a war was something the union, management, and especially the politicians didn't want on their hands. Your father made noise until, one day, someone paid him a visit. Real tough bastards, those two were."

The blue eyes glistened. Emotion or rage, I couldn't distinguish which.

"Insurance doesn't pay out on a suicide, but you know that from your work as a PI. No widow's benefit meant you had to drop out of that school."

"St. Wystan's," I said, numb as I recall life after the death of my father.

I had walked into the room. My father was on the sofa, his head tilted back, mouth open, and his blood and brains splattered on the wall behind him. All that blood had ruined the wallpaper, dripped down, and soaked the carpet. The revolver was on the floor. Jimmy's voice snapped me out of the macabre reverie.

"They forced him to write a brief note and then had him pull the trigger."

My eyes focused. "Those two guys...are they still alive?"

"Put one down for a heart attack. The other one is still alive, in a nursing home, fucked up from a stroke. He's on a diet of Gerber baby food, in diapers, and stares at a wall all day. I'd like to think he is screaming inside his own head, and nobody but him can hear it. Some call it ironic, but to me, it's poetic."

"What about those who ordered it?" I asked.

"Now we're talking." Jimmy held up a finger. "One guy, and his name is like a song on the show Top of the Pops; it's all there on that piece of paper, on top of your money."

I stood up. I couldn't feel my legs. I looked down at the stack, now aware of the note that Jimmy talked about. I saw the writing. He'd written three names. He had put a line through one name due to a heart attack. It was all there in neat, legible cursive. I read the name of number two and the address for the nursing home. The remaining name, like the song Harry Nilsson had written but the band Three Dog Night made famous, "One is the Loneliest Number," stood there, waiting for me.

"And what do you expect me to do with this, Jimmy?"

"Information is for you to spend any which way you choose. I couldn't care less."

I could swear I saw a twinkle in his eyes, like it was some Technicolor special effect.

"You're not me, but if I were you, I'd pay the vegetable a visit. I'd let the bastard see me. Let him have a taste of terror instead of strained peas. Then, I don't know. It's a nursing home, so I'd get creative." He smiled. "I can't help but think of those soap operas on television. Ma watched them all the time. There was always a character in a coma, someone bedridden, and they were done in with an air embolism, you know, a bubble of air in their IV." He snapped his fingers. "A little air works like a depth charge to the brain or the lungs." Jimmy imitated the sound of a small explosion.

He looked at me. "Me? I'd let the bastard suffer a little. I crimp the tubing to his air tank. I'd do a little stop and go until he stopped breathing, but knowing my luck, there's monitors everywhere."

I held up the stack of money. "Thanks for this, Jimmy. Won't say it's been a pleasure, but it's been something."

"It has, Shane Cleary. That something is called revelation, the truth."

I pocketed the money, which was worthless to me at this point. I moved numb, but my mind wanted me to sprint the hell out of there. Every memory I had of my father rushed to me. Integrity is what got my father killed.

I wished my younger self had been there to stop those two men. I had so many unanswered questions. Could he have shot one of them and overpowered the other one? Had there been more than one bullet in the chamber? I left Jimmy and his dog behind me. I walked past the kid unpacking boxes, walked through a veil of stale dust and cigarette smoke.

The big lie.

Chapter Twenty-Seven: Catch

The revelation cycled and recycled through my head. Stunned, angry, and ill after the meet with Jimmy, my feet moved me home, where I used the railing to climb up to Bonnie's bedroom. She wanted to celebrate her victory, or rather, 'our' victory, with a special dinner. Her treat. I said 'rain check.' She asked what was wrong, and I lied about a bad headache. I petted Delilah and then fed her.

My father had survived combat in the Pacific theatre. He would see action again in the First Battle of Naktong Bulge during the early days of the Korean Conflict. I would learn from a family friend that he had seen the bodies of American servicemen massacred at Hill 303. He had experienced the extremes of deprivation, whether it was food and water or heat and cold. Both were hell for any soldier. To have survived all that and then to have been forced to blow his brains out made me sick.

The next day, I picked up a cake for Silvia's birthday in the North End. I stopped in at Vittoria's for a coffee and sat at a table to enjoy it. I considered the unnecessary cruelty of what had been done to my father and then to my mother and me. The life insurance policy. I'm talking about the clause some smart lawyer weaved into the pages of legalese that permitted the company and employer to refuse payment to the widow of a suicide. It was the salt that killed everything, so nothing would grow.

They were Rome, and we were Carthage.

Avarice. Pride.

I was in the shade of my own thoughts when the shadow of Tony Two-Times darkened the marble tabletop. "For you," he said.

He pulled out a small brown bag, its top rolled and pinched tight, the way Mom handed out lunches. He set it next to the boxed cake. He walked away to find a private table. I unrolled the top and peeked inside at the impromptu present.

A bag of dog treats. Code from Mr. B that business was business.

No hard feelings that I'd taken a gig from a mutual enemy.

When I finished my espresso, I realized I had forgotten to call Bill with the results from the research on his beau. I located a pay phone on a wall, dropped in some change, and dialed his number. I told him that his new boyfriend Tony had come up clean in the wash. The man had one hidden secret. We all do. He was embarrassed that he had not finished high school.

Bonnie and I went to Silvia's party later that day. John pulled me aside soon after our arrival to tell me that the Irish shakedowns had stopped. He clapped me on the back before he returned to the role of host. Bill arrived, introduced me to Tony Acosta. Heads turned. There were the usual whispers about a man too handsome, too gorgeous not to be straight. Bill asked me my opinion, and I told him I was happy for him. I made small talk, asked him the usual about work. He sipped, winked, and walked away.

Silvia put out a delicious spread of soul food. We ate. Everyone drank. Some danced while others retired to chairs or sofas for conversation. The professor was on the far side of the room playing a game of Charades. I worked the room. I shopped the same smile and the same expression. Every now and then, I'd catch a glance from Bonnie.

At some point, I checked my watch for the time. I stood near a window that overlooked the street. I swept aside the curtain and observed life below from that height. Down there were figures I couldn't make out walking out into the middle of the asphalt, but as they came into view, I could see that one was younger and the other older. There was no traffic. No sooner had they stopped and stood still in the dusk than a street lamp flickered and burst bright with white light. The two of them looked up in amazement. The boy pointed to the light. The man smiled and talked. When a hand moved, a ball was released. I watched it arc and land into waiting hands. Back and forth in a hypnotic sway, I watched them play catch. I watched until there was nothing but throw and catch, the soft sounds of their exchange that needed neither words nor applause. I watched a father and son. I watched.

I fought back a single tear.

Acknowledgements

I'm grateful to my publisher, Level Best Books, for their continued faith in Shane Cleary. Thank you, Dames of Detection.

Hugs and friendship for Shawn Reilly Simmons, my editor.

I'm thankful for the generosity and feedback from my proofreaders Dean Hunt and continuity editor Deb Well. I'm especially thankful to fellow author Tina deBellegarde who proofread the manuscript. They made Shane Cleary better on the page.

A word of thanks to Marie Sultana Robinson who introduced me to Nonantum on Facebook, and for her unique slices of life during the Seventies. Andrew Slipp has provided me with invaluable guidance and observations from his own life during the decade.

As always, nothing but gratitude to my fellow Level Best authors, and to friends of the pen and keyboard in crime fiction, the best and most supportive community around for a writer.

Until Shane appears again, thank you.

About the Author

Gabriel Valjan is the Agatha, Anthony, Derringer, Silver Falchion and Shamus nominated author of the Shane Cleary mystery series with Level Best Books. He received the 2021 Macavity Award for Best Short Story. Gabriel is a member of ITW, MWA, and Sisters in Crime. He is a regular contributor to the Criminal Minds blog. He lives in Boston's South End and answers to a tuxedo cat named Munchkin.

SOCIAL MEDIA HANDLES:
  Instagram: @gabrielvaljan
  Twitter: @GValjan

AUTHOR WEBSITE:
  gabrielvaljan.com

Also by Gabriel Valjan

Shane Cleary Mystery Series
Liar's Dice
Hush Hush
Symphony Road
Dirty Old Town

Company Files Series
The Devil's Music
The Naming Game
The Good Man

Milton Keynes UK
Ingram Content Group UK Ltd.
UKHW010641040324
438885UK00001B/182